AF261304

ARTIST'S INTRODUCTION

As a young reader, I was obsessed
with the Commonplace Book. Having
devoured H.P. Lovecraft's most
well-known stories, I began hunt-
ing down his lesser work, even his
revisions of other authors. I found
mentions & references to the Commonplace Book, but I could never
find a copy.

Later, I discovered that the pub-
lishers of Lovecraft"s correspondence included the Commonplace Book
in some collections as almost an
addendum; this journal of story
ideas in short sentences, sometimes
paragraphs or notes on stories by
other authors--all jumping-off
points for future work. As an ill-
ustrator, the entries reminded me
of a sketchbook; in a rush, you
scribble something down to revisit
it for a deeper exploration later.
I know Lovecraft intended to look

back upon it for source material,
but what enticed me was its poten-
tial for other artists & writers.
It's like a collection of improv
prompts or art school illustration
cues. One of my favorite things is
 when multiple artists illustrate
the same source & seeing the results! Something about it also re-
minds me of a dungeon master's
roughly jotted-down notes for their
adventurers & what they'll encount-
er during gameplay.

As some of you may know, I've drawn
a lot of work inspired by Lovecraft
over the years, including creatures
from the Commonplace Book. My idea
for this new version was to approach
each prompt as freshly as possible,
ignoring what I had already designed.
In some cases, that didn't work &
my original ideas/concepts turned
out to be the best.

If you're a writer, artist or just a fan
of Lovecraft's work, I hope you find
this book entertaining & inspiring.

This book consists of ideas, images, & quotations hastily jotted down for possible future use in weird fiction. Very few are actually developed plots--for the most part they are merely suggestions or random impressions designed to set the memory or imagination working. Their sources are various--dreams, things read, casual incidents, idle conceptions, & so on.

--H.P. Lovecraft

Presented to R.H.Barlow, Esq. on May 7, 1934--in exchange for an admirably neat typed copy from his skilled hand.

Demophon

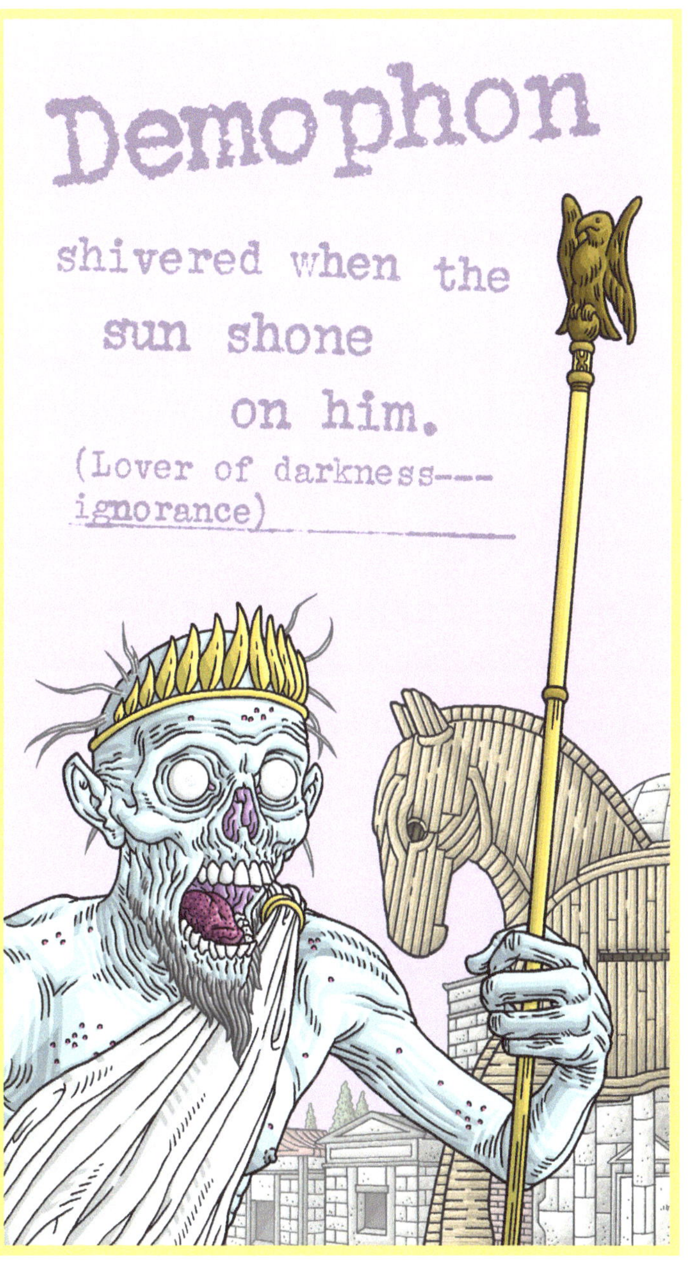

N.E. region called "Witches
     Hollow" - along course of a
river. Rumours of witches'
     sabbaths & Indian powwows
on a broad round mound rising out of the level, where
some old hemlocks & beeches
formed a dark grove or daemon-
temple. Legends hard to acc-
ount for. Holmes-Guardian An-
     gel.
____

Witches' Hollow (novel ?) Man
hired as teacher in private
school misses road on first
trip- encounters dark hollow
with unnaturally swollen trees
     & small cottage (light in
     window ?) Reaches school
& hears that boys are forbidden to visit hollow. One
     boys is strange- teacher
sees him visit hollow- odd
doings- mysterious dis-
appearance or hideous fate.
____
                    Celephaïs
Dream of flying over city.
____

4

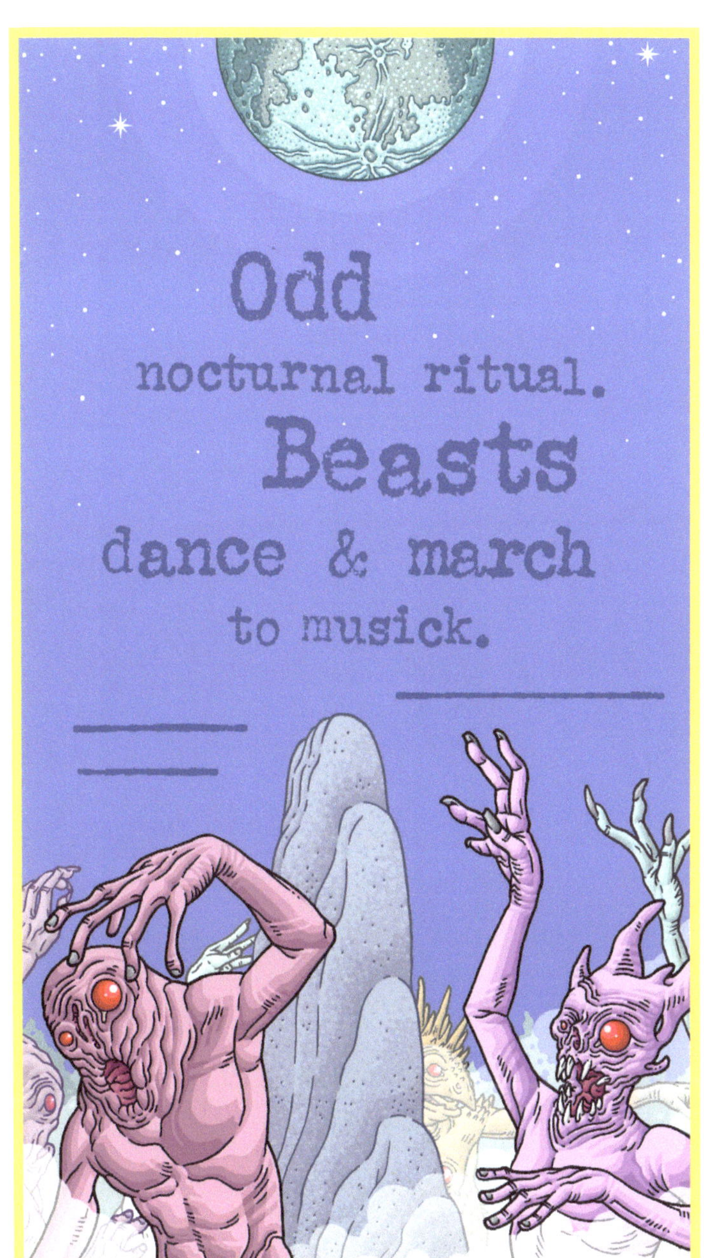

Odd
nocturnal ritual.
Beasts
dance & march
to musick.

Dream of Seekonk-ebbing
tide- bolt from sky- exodus
from Providence-fall of ⚡
Congregational dome.

Strange visit to a place at
night-moonlight-castle of
great magnificence &c.
Daylight shows either aban-
donment or unrecognisable
ruins..perhaps of vast antiquity.

Moving away from earth more
swiftly than light. Past gra-
dually unfolded-horrible revelation.

Determinism & prophecy.

Sounds ..possibly musical..
heard in the night from
other worlds or realms or
being.

Horror Story The sculptured
hand--or other artificial
hand--which strangles
its creator.

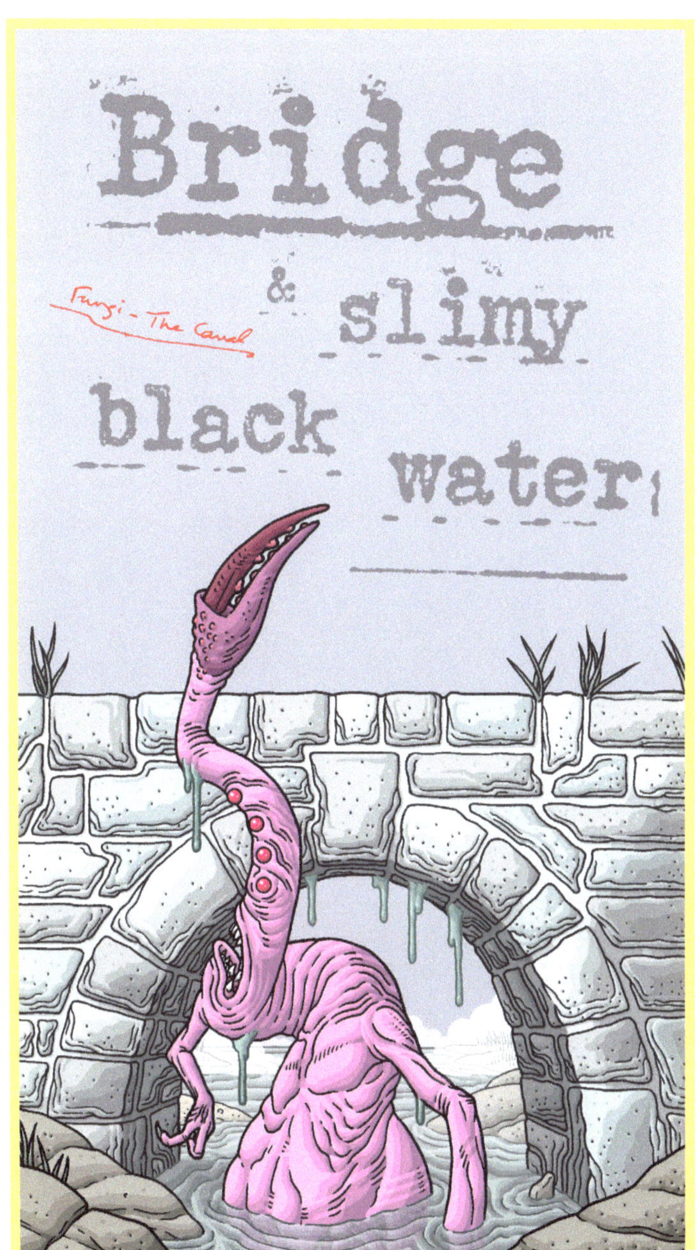

Bridge
& slimy
black
water
Fungi – The Canal

In an ancient buried city a
man finds a mouldering pre-
    historic document in English
in his own handwriting tellin
an incredible tale. Voyage
    from present into past im
plied. Possible actualisa-
    tion of this.   ~~used 1935~~

        Time & space- past ev-
    ent- 150 years ago- unex-
plained. Modern period- person
    intensely homesick for past
says or does something which
    is physically transmitted
back & actually causes the
        past event.

Certain kind of deep-toned
    stately music of the style of
the 1870's or 1880's recalls

certain visions of that per-
iod-- gas-litten parlours
of the dead, moonlight on old
    floors, decaying business

        streets with gas lamps
&c- under terrible circum-
        stances.

<u>Hand of dead man writes.</u>
Lonely bleak islands of NE coast. Horrors they harbor— <u>outpost of cosmic influence.</u>

The Cats of Ulthar The cat is the soul of antique Ægyptus & bearer of tales from forgotten cities of Meroë & Ophir. He is the kin of the jungle's lords & heir to the secrets of hoary & sinister Africa. The Sphinx is his cousin, & he speaks her language; but he is more ancient than the Sphinx & remembers that which she hath forgotten.

Man enters (supposedly)
own house in pitch dark. Feels
way to room and shuts door behind him. Strange horrors— or
turns on light & finds alien
place or presence. Or finds
past restored or future indi-
cated.

Pane of peculiar-looking
glass from a ruined monastery
reputed to have harbou ed
devil-worship set up in
modern house at edge of wild
country. Landscape looks
vaguely & unplacably wrong
through it. It has some unknown time-distorting quality
& comes from a primal lost
civilisation. Finally, hideous thing in other world
seen through it.

Lone lagoons & swamps of
Louisiana—death daemon—
ancient house & gardens—
moss- grown trees- festoons of
Spanish moss.

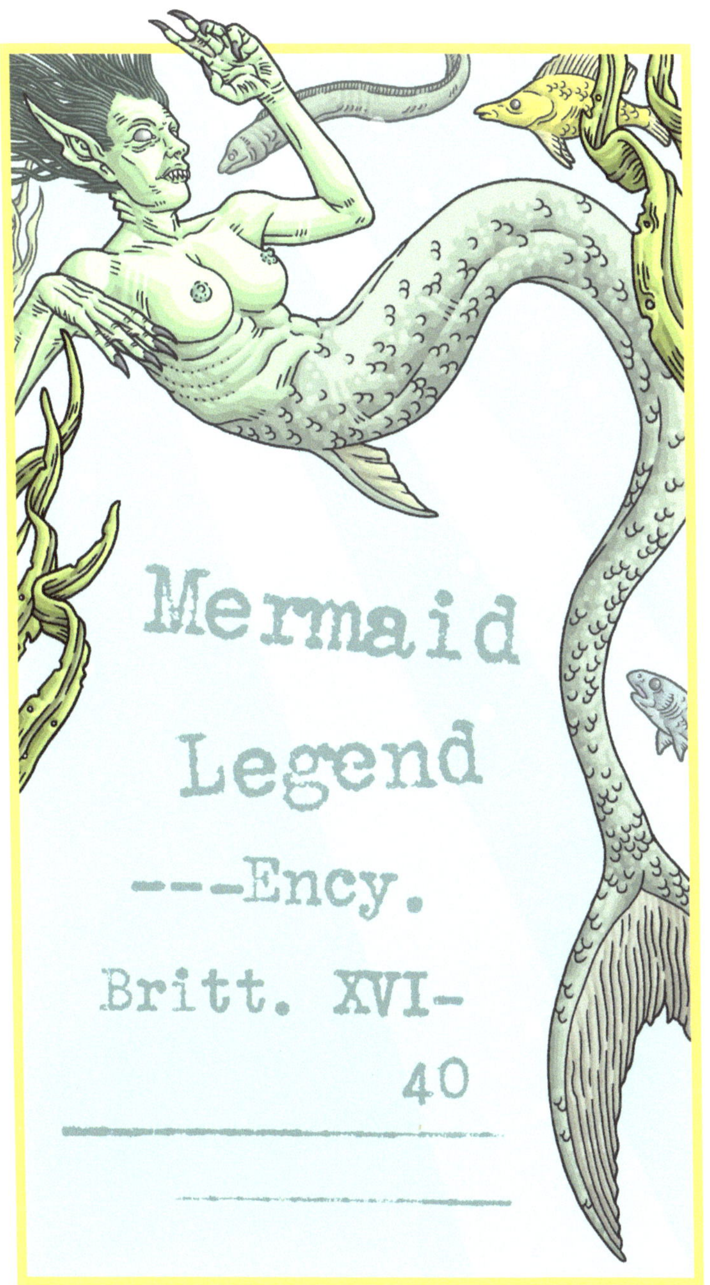

Mermaid
Legend
---Ency.
Britt. XVI-
40

Thing from sea-in dark house-
man finds doorknobs &c _wet_
as from touch of _something_.
He has been a sea-captain, &
once found a strange temple
      on a volcanically risen
      island.

   Murder discovered- body
located by psychological
detective who pretends
he has made walls of room
transparent. Works on fear
of murderer..

Man with unnatural face--oddit
of speaking--found to be a
mask. Revelation.

Man has sold soul to devil-
returns to family from
trip-life afterward- fear-
culminating horror- novel
length ?

Identity--reconstruction of
personality--man makes dupli-
cate of himself.

Phleg'ee-thon--a river of
      liquid fire in Hades.

Expedition lost in
Antarctic or other
weird place. Skele-
     tons & effects
found years later.
   Camera films used
but undeveloped.
Finders deve-   xxxxx
     lope & find strange horror.

A very ancient colossus in a
very ancient desert. Face
gone--no man hath seen it.

The man who would not sleep--
dares not sleep--takes drugs
to keep himself awake.
Finally falls asleep--- &
something happens.   [happens]
   Motto from Baudelaire p. 214.

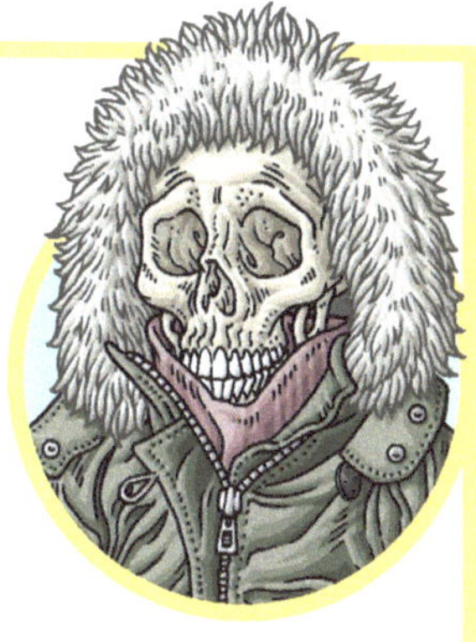

Dunsany--(Go-By street) Man
stumbles on dream-world-
   returns to Earth---seeks t
to go back---succeeds , but
finds dream-world ancient &
decayed as though by thou-
sands of years.

Sealed room--or at least no
lamp allowed there.
Shadow on wall.

Any very ancient, unknown, or
prehistoric object- its power
of suggestion- forbidden mem-
ories.

Evil alley or enclosed court
in ancient city

Visit to someone in wild &
remote house- ride from sta-
tion through the night- into
the haunted hills- houses by
forest or water- terrible
things live there.

Man forced to take shelter in
strange house. Host has
thick beard & dark glasses.
Retires. In night guest rises
& sees host's clothes about
- also mask which was the a-
pparent face of whatever the
host was. Flight.

Trophonius- cave of. Vide
Class. Dict. & Atlantic article.

Life & .Death

Death..its desolation &
horror..bleak spaces..sea-
bottom..dead cities.

But life!
The greater horror! Vast un-
heard-of reptiles & levithans
& hideous beasts of prehistoric jungle...rank slimy vege
tation- evil instincts of
primal man-

Life is more
horrible
than
Death.

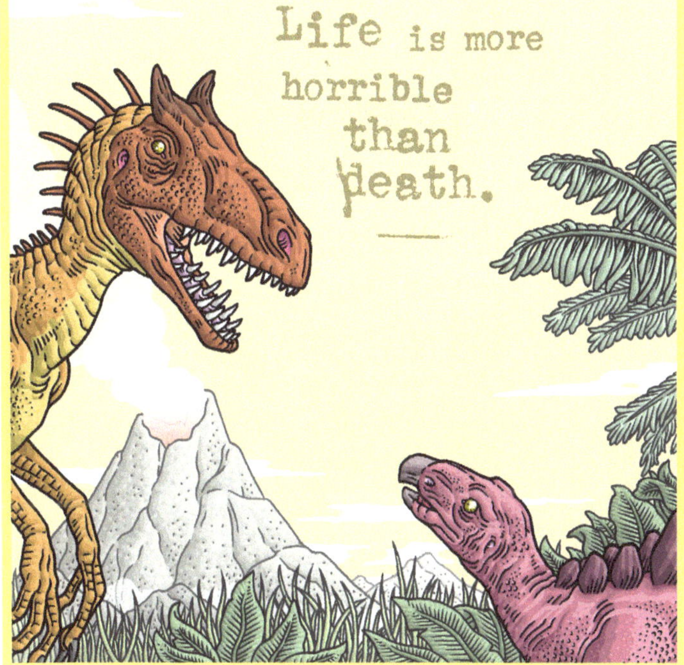

Cities wiped out by supernatural wrath.

Italian revenge-killing self
in cell with enemy--under
castle.

The walking dead--seemingly
alive, but--

Calamander-wood--- a very
valuable wood of Ceylon &
S. India, resembling
rosewood.

Revise 1907 tale - painting of
ultimate horror.

Monsters born living--burrow
underground & multiply, forming
race of unsuspected daemons.

Wall paper cracks off in
sinister shape--man dies
of fright. Rats in Wall

Hideous secret society--wide
spread--horrible rites in
caverns under familiar scenes--
one's own neighbor may belong.

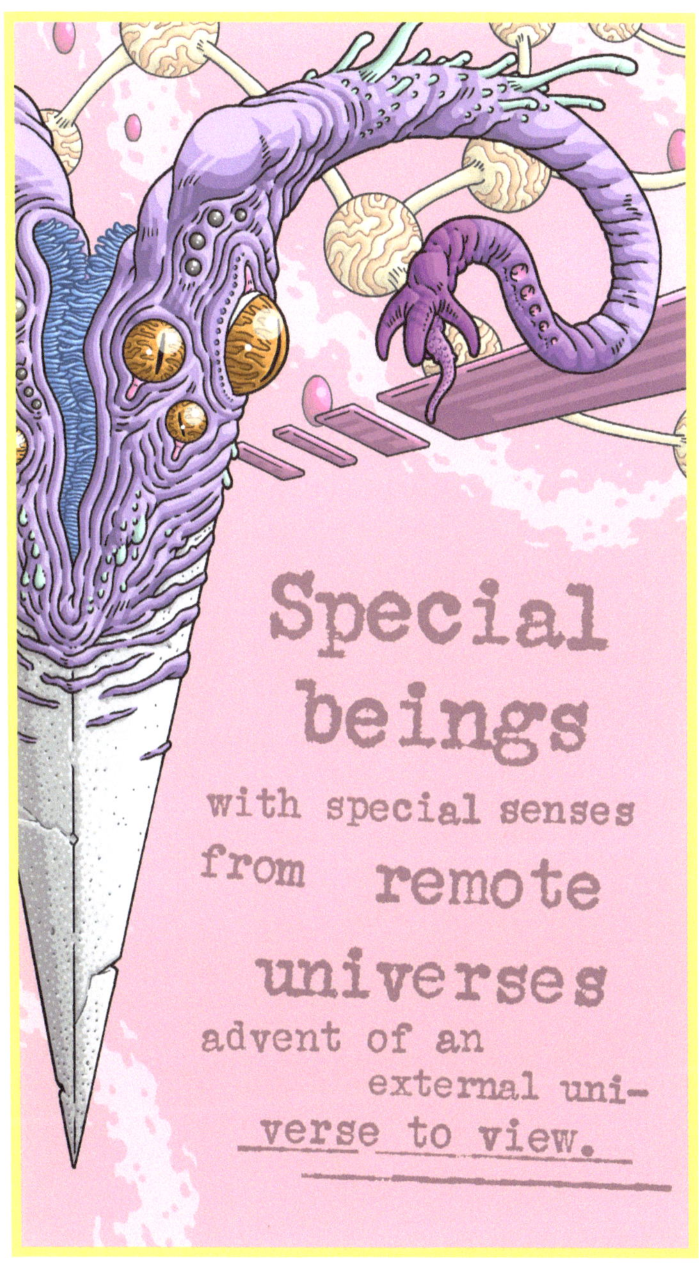

Special
beings
with special senses
from   remote

universes
advent of an
external uni-
verse to view.

Footnote by Haggard or Lang
in THE WORLD'S DESIRE.

"Probably the mysterious &
indecipherable ancient books,
which were occasionally exca-
vated in old Egypt, were writ-
ten in this dead language of a
more ancient & now forgotten
    people. Such was the book
    discovered at Coptos, in
the sanctuary there, by a
priest of the goddess. 'The
whole earth was dark, but the
moon shone all about the Book'
A scribe of the period of the
    Ramessids mentions another in
        indecipherable ancient
        writing. ' Thou tellest me
thou understandest no word of
it , good or bad. There is, as
it were, a wall about it that
none may climb. Thou art in-
structed , yet thou knowest it
not; this makes me afraid."'
    Birch Zeitschrift 1871 pp
61-64 Papyrus Anastasi I pl X
1.8. pl X 1.4 Maspero Hist.
    Anc. pp 66-67.

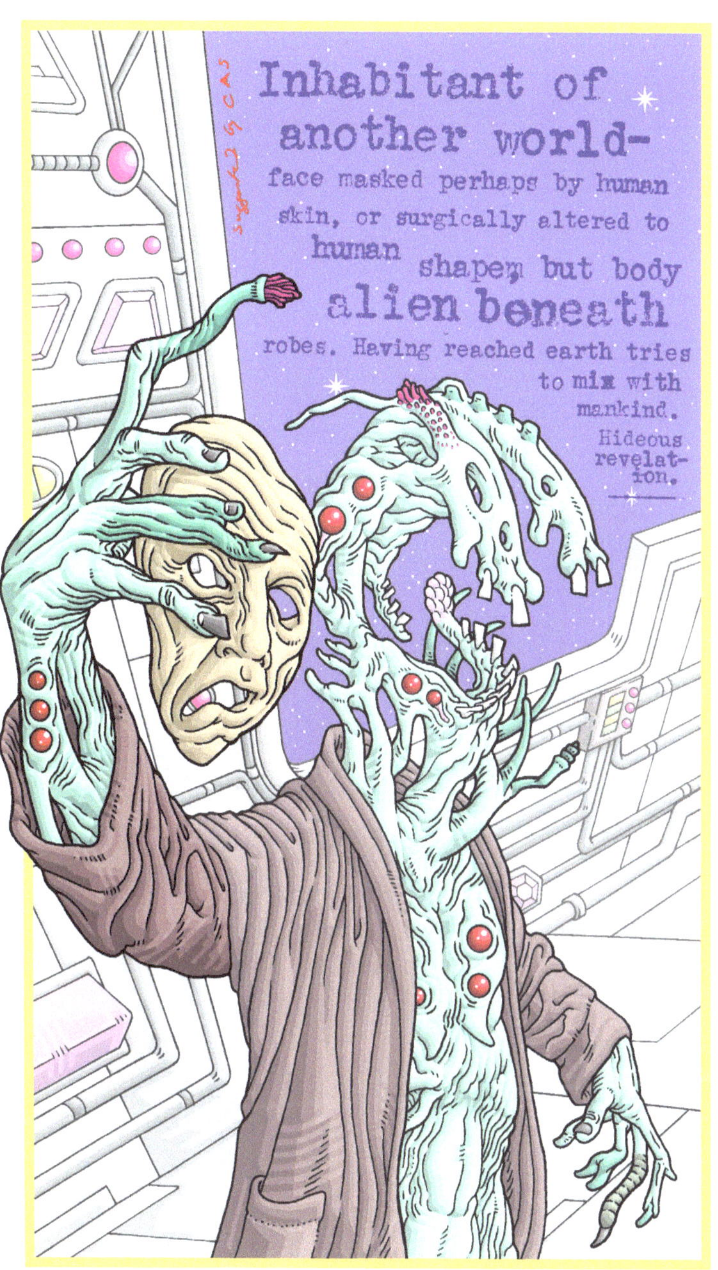

Inhabitant of another world—
face masked perhaps by human skin, or surgically altered to human shape, but body alien beneath robes. Having reached earth tries to mix with mankind. Hideous revelation.

A secret living thing kept &
    fed in an old house.

    Horrible things whispered
in the lines of Gauther de
Metz (13th cent.) IMAGE DU
MONDE.

Man makes appt. with old
enemy . Dies---body keeps
appt.

Talking bird of
great long-
    evity-
tells secret long
after ward.

Dried-up man living for cen-
turies in cataleptic state
in ancient tomb.

    Photius tells of a (lost)
writer named Damascius,
    who wrote INCREDIBLE FICTIONS
        TALES OF DAEMONS
    MARVELLOUS STORIES OF APPEAR-
    ANCES FROM THE DEAD.

The Italians call
Fear La figlia
della Mote---
--- the
daughter of
Death

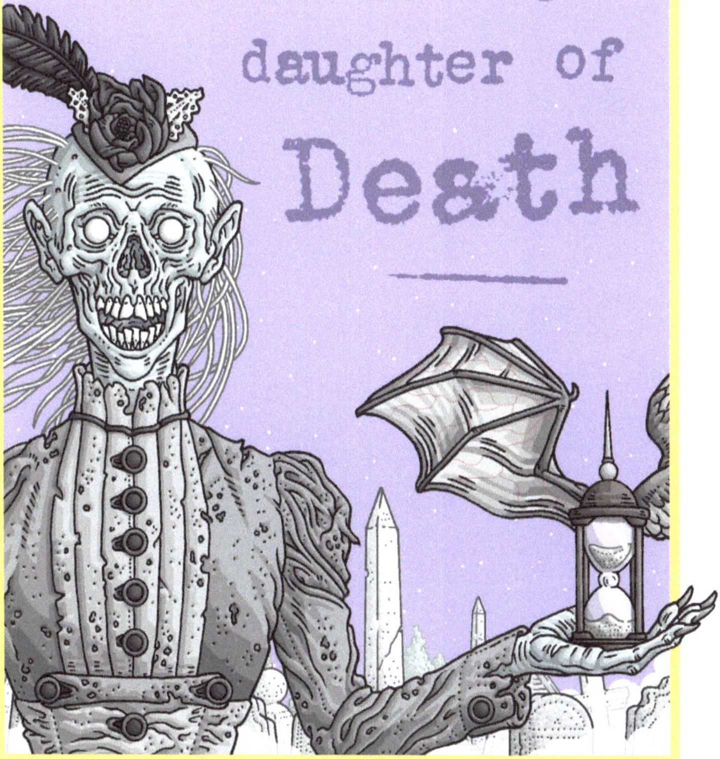

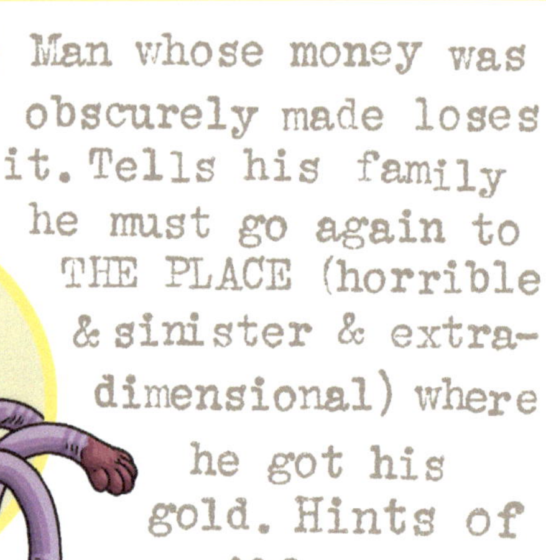

Man whose money was obscurely made loses it. Tells his family he must go again to THE PLACE (horrible & sinister & extra-dimensional) where he got his gold. Hints of possible pursuers ——or of possible non-return. He goes——— record of what happens to him——or what happens at his home when he returns. Perhaps connect with ensuing topic. Give fantastic, quasi-<u>Dunsanian</u> treatment.

Ultimate horror———grandfather returns from strange trip———mystery in house——wind & darkness———grandf. & mother engulfed———questions

forbidden ---somnolence
---investigation---
cataclysm---screams over-
heard.

Man observed in a public
place with features (or
ring or jewel) identi-
fied with those of man
long (perhaps genera-
tions) buried.

Terrible trip to an
ancient & forgotten tomb.

Strange book of horror discovered in ancient library.
Paragraphs of terrible sig-
nificance copied. Later un-
able to find book & verify
text. Perhaps discover
body or image or charm under
floor, in secret cupboard,
or elsewhere. Idea that book
was merely hypnotic delusion
induced by dead brain or ancient magic.

Thibetan ROLANG— Sorcerer
(or NGAGSPA) reanimates a
corpse by holding it in a dark
room— lying on it mouth
to mouth & repeating a magic
formula with all else banish-
ed from his mind. Corpse
comes slowly to life & stands
up. Tries to escape & leaps
& bounds & struggles— but
sorcerer holds it & contin-
ues with magic formula. Corpse
sticks out tongue &
sorcerer bites it
off. Corpse then
collapses. Tongue
becomes a valuable
magic talisman.
If corpse escapes—
hideous results &
death to sorcerer.

Man blindfolded & taken in
closed cab to some very ancient & secret place.

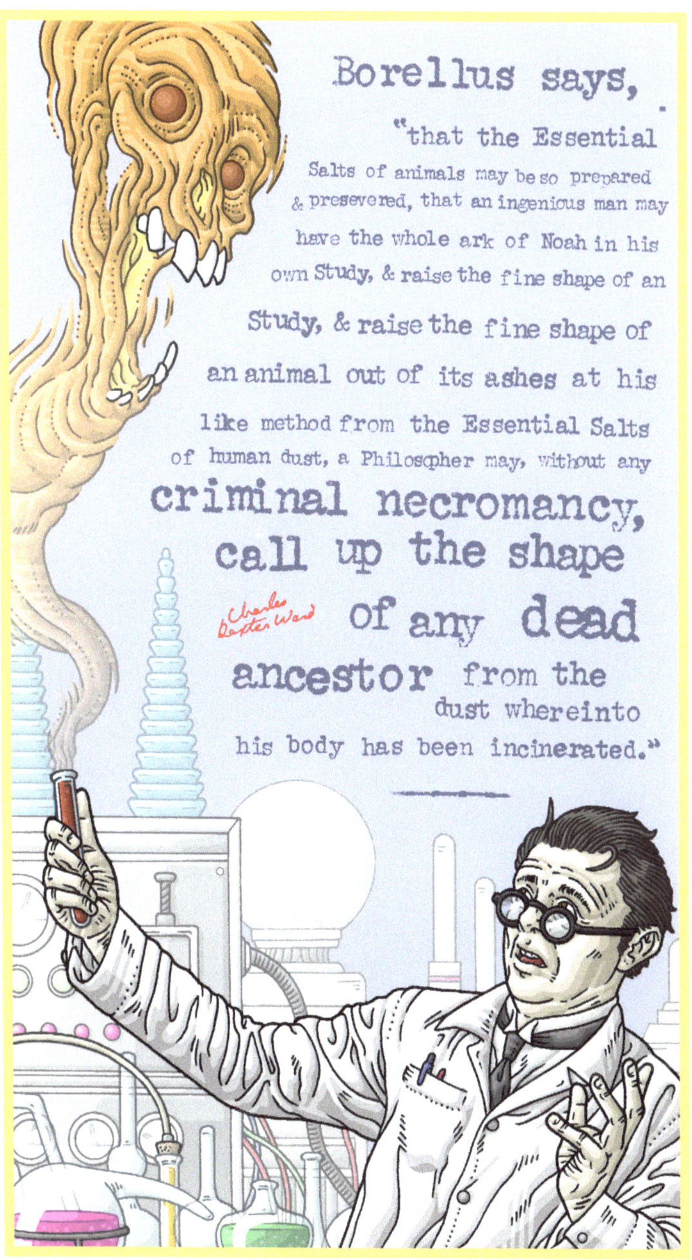

Borellus says,
"that the Essential
Salts of animals may be so prepared
& presevered, that an ingenious man may
have the whole ark of Noah in his
own Study, & raise the fine shape of an
Study, & raise the fine shape of
an animal out of its ashes at his
like method from the Essential Salts
of human dust, a Philosopher may, without any
criminal necromancy,
call up the shape
of any dead
ancestor from the
dust whereinto
his body has been incinerated."
Charles Dexter Ward

Man's body dies— but corpse
retains life. Stalks about —
  tries to conceal odour of
decay detained somewhere—
hideous climax.   Cool Air
Unknown fires seen across the
    hills at night.

    A place one has been— a
beautiful view of village or
farm-dotted valley in the sun-
set— which one cannot find
  again or locate in memory.
  Change comes over sun— shows
objects in strange form, perhaps restoring landscape
of the past.

4/2   Lost winter day—slept
        over— 20 years later.

    Sleep in armchair summer
night— false dawn— old
  scenery & sensations— cold-
old persons now dead— horror-
  frozen ?

    anencephalous or brain-
less monster who survives &
attains prodigious size.

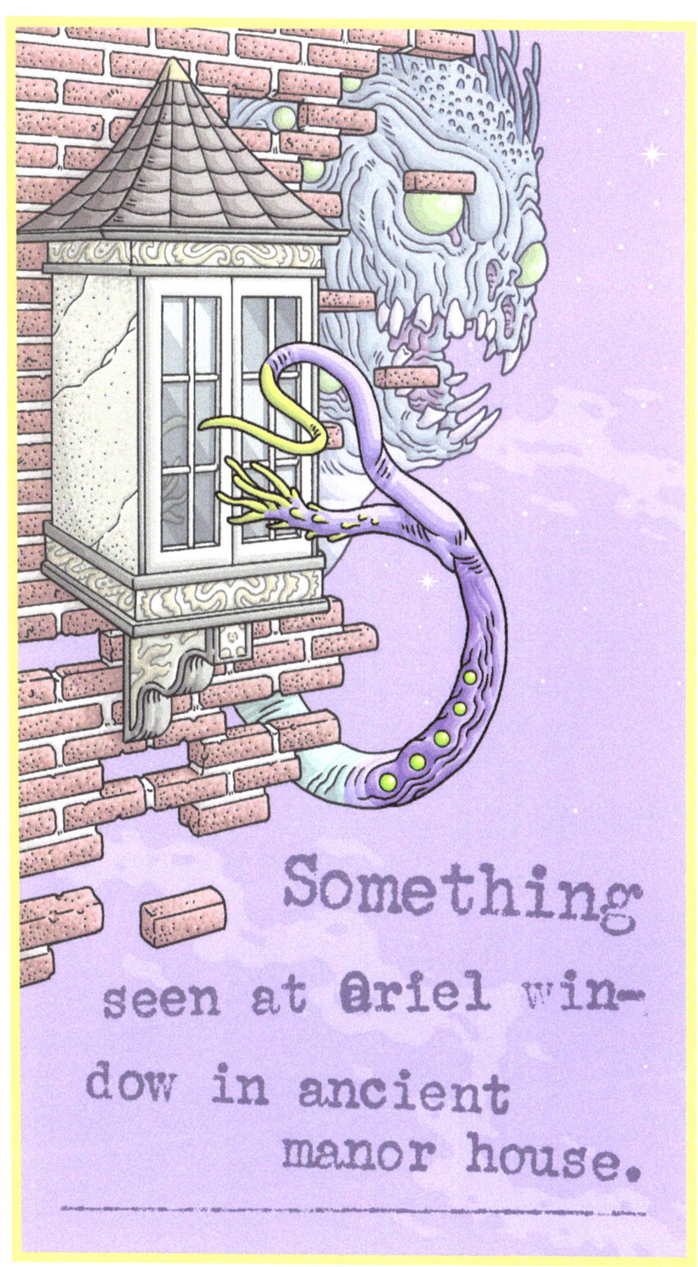

Something seen at oriel window in ancient manor house.

Desert of rock - prehis-
toric door in cliff, in
the valley around which lie the
bones of uncounted billions
of animals both modern & prehistoric; some of them puzz-
lingly gnawed.

Scene of an urban horror----
Sousle Cap or Champlain Sts,
Quebec $\frac{3}{4}$ rugged cliff-face-
moss, mildew, dampness-
houses half-burrowing in-
to cliff.

Dream of awakening in vast
hall of strange architecture,
with sheet-covered forms on
slabs- in positions similar
to one's own. Suggestions of
disturbingly non-human out-
lines under sheets. One of
the objects moves & throws
off sheet- non-terrestrial
being revealed. Sugg. that
oneself is such a being- mind
has become transferred to
body on other planet.

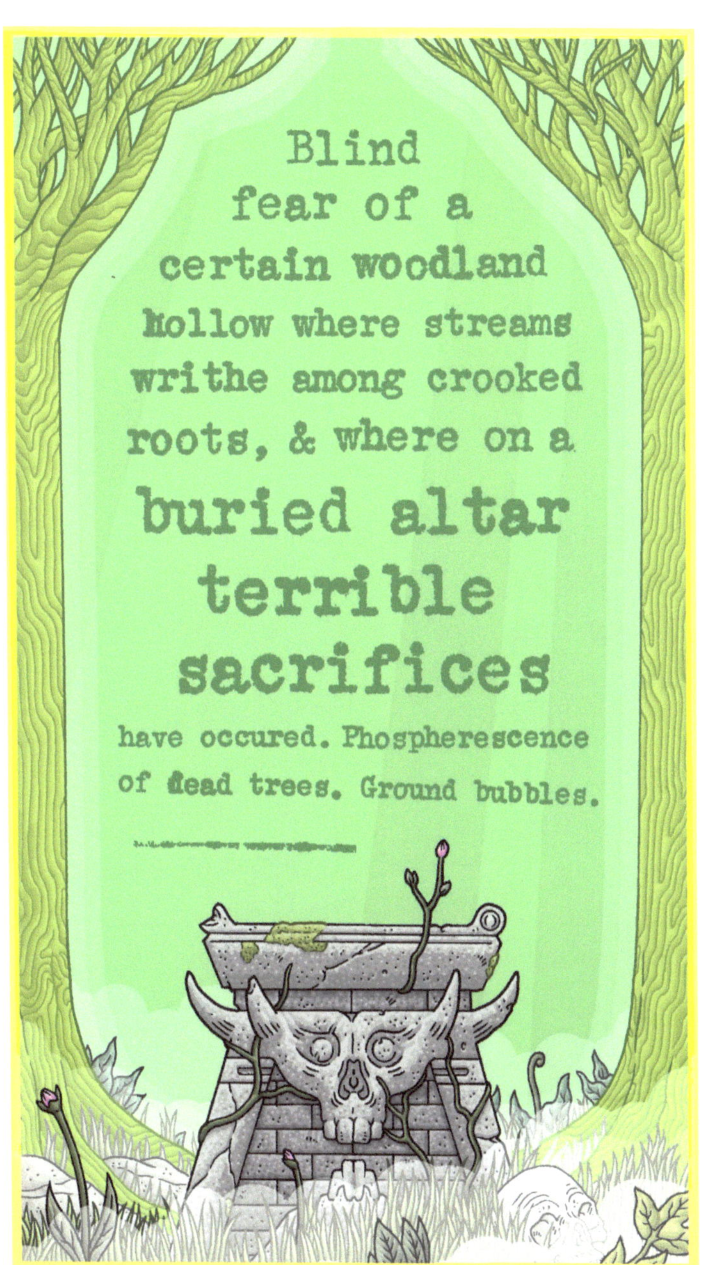

Blind fear of a certain woodland hollow where streams writhe among crooked roots, & where on a buried altar terrible sacrifices have occured. Phospherescence of dead trees. Ground bubbles.

Man visits museum of antiqui-
ties--asks that it accept a
bas-relief he has just made--
old & learned curator laughs
& says he cannot accept any-
thing so modern. Man says that
'dreams are older than brood-
ing Egypt or the contempla-
tive Sphinx or garden-girdled
Babylonia' & that he had
fashioned the sculpture in his
dreams. Curator bids him
shew his product, & when he
does so curator shews horror.
Asks who the man may be. He
tells modern name. "No--before
that" says curator. Man does
not remember except in
dreams. Then curator offers
high price, but man fears he
means to destroy sculpture.
Asks fabulous price--curator
will consult directors. Add
good development & describe
nature of bas-relief.

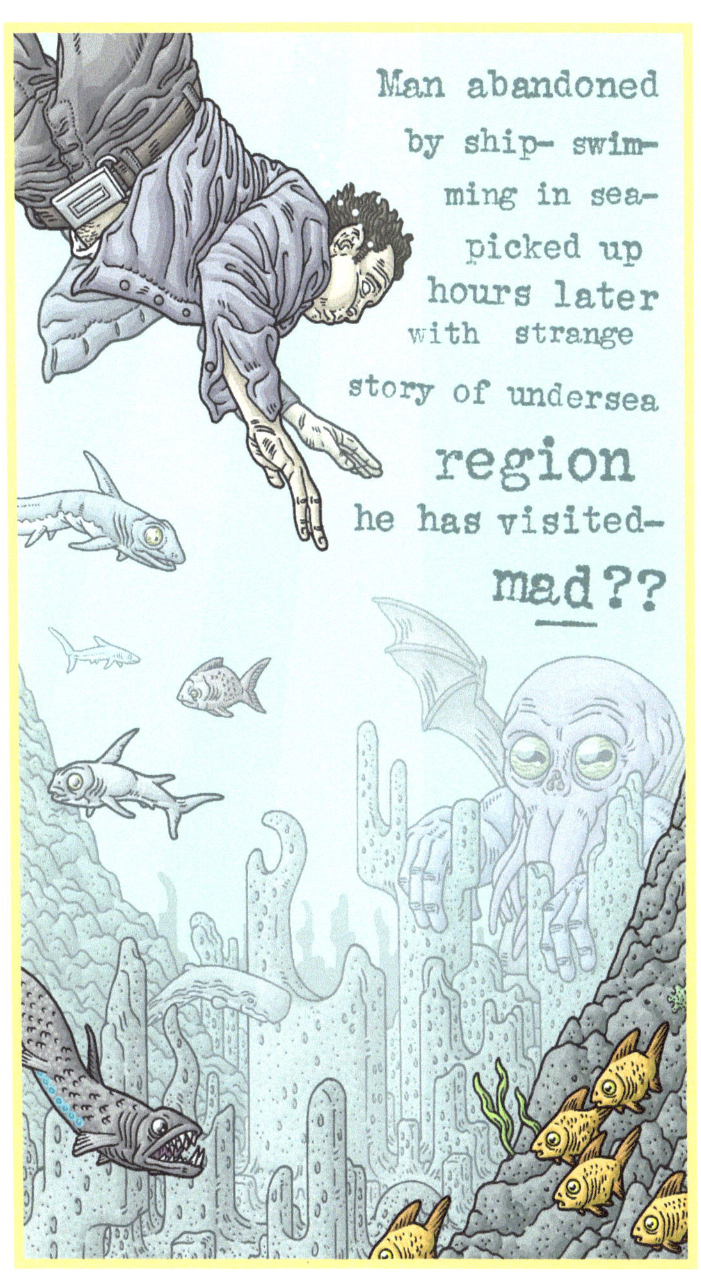

Man abandoned
by ship- swim-
ming in sea-
picked up
hours later
with strange
story of undersea
region
he has visited-
mad??

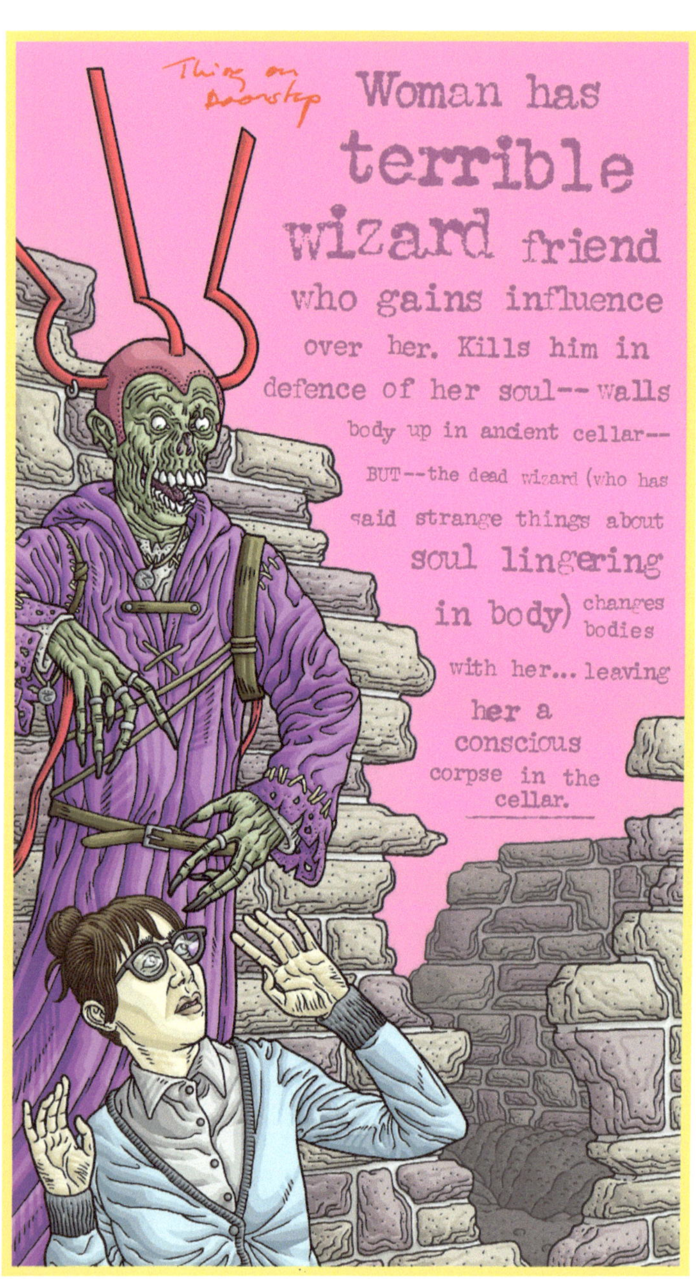

Thing on Doorstep
Woman has terrible wizard friend who gains influence over her. Kills him in defence of her soul-- walls body up in ancient cellar-- BUT--the dead wizard (who has said strange things about soul lingering in body) changes bodies with her... leaving her a conscious corpse in the cellar.

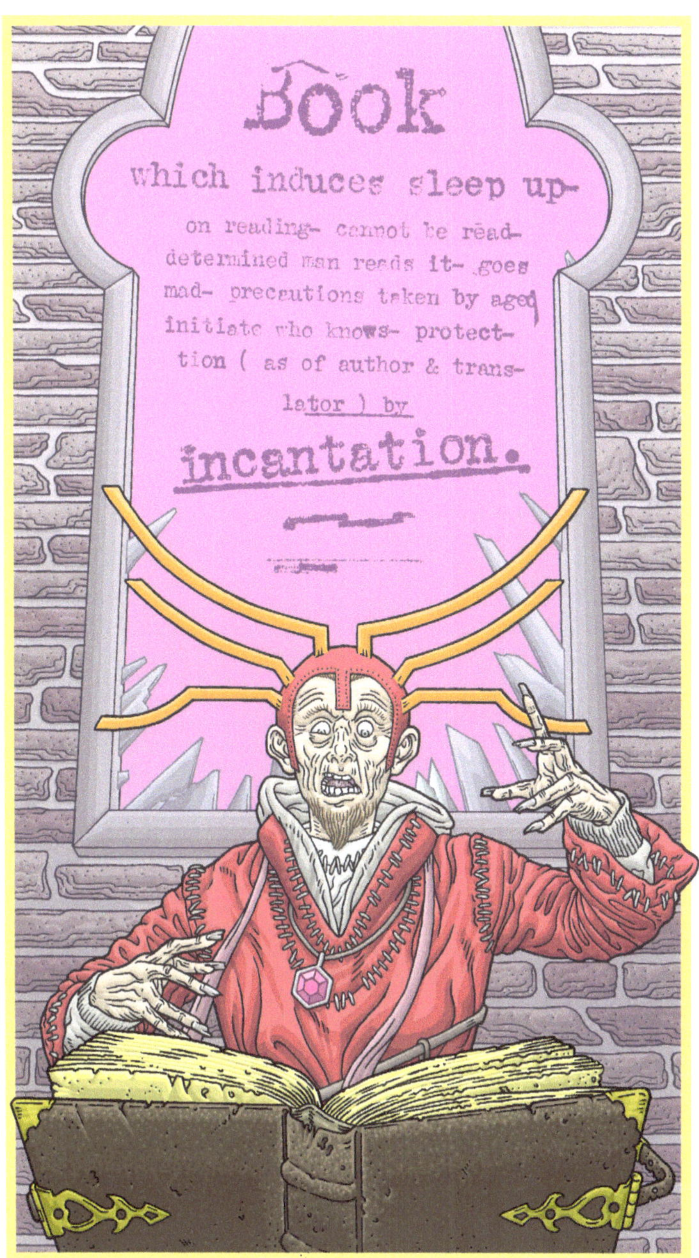
BOOK
which induces sleep up-
on reading- cannot be read-
determined man reads it- goes
mad- precautions taken by aged
initiate who knows- protect-
tion (as of author & trans-
lator) by
incantation.

Quoted as motto by John
Buchan.

" The effect of night, of
any flowing water, of the
peep of day, of ships, of
the open ocean, calls up
in the mind an army of
anonymous desires & plea-
sures. Something, we
feel, should happen; we
know not what, yet we pro-
ceed in quest of it."

R.L.Stevenson

Unspeakable dance of the
gargoyles- in morning
several gargoyles on old
cathedral found transposed.

Wandering through labyrinth
of narrow slum streets- come
on distant light-unheardof
rites of swarming beggars-
like Court of Miracles du
Notre Dame de Paris.

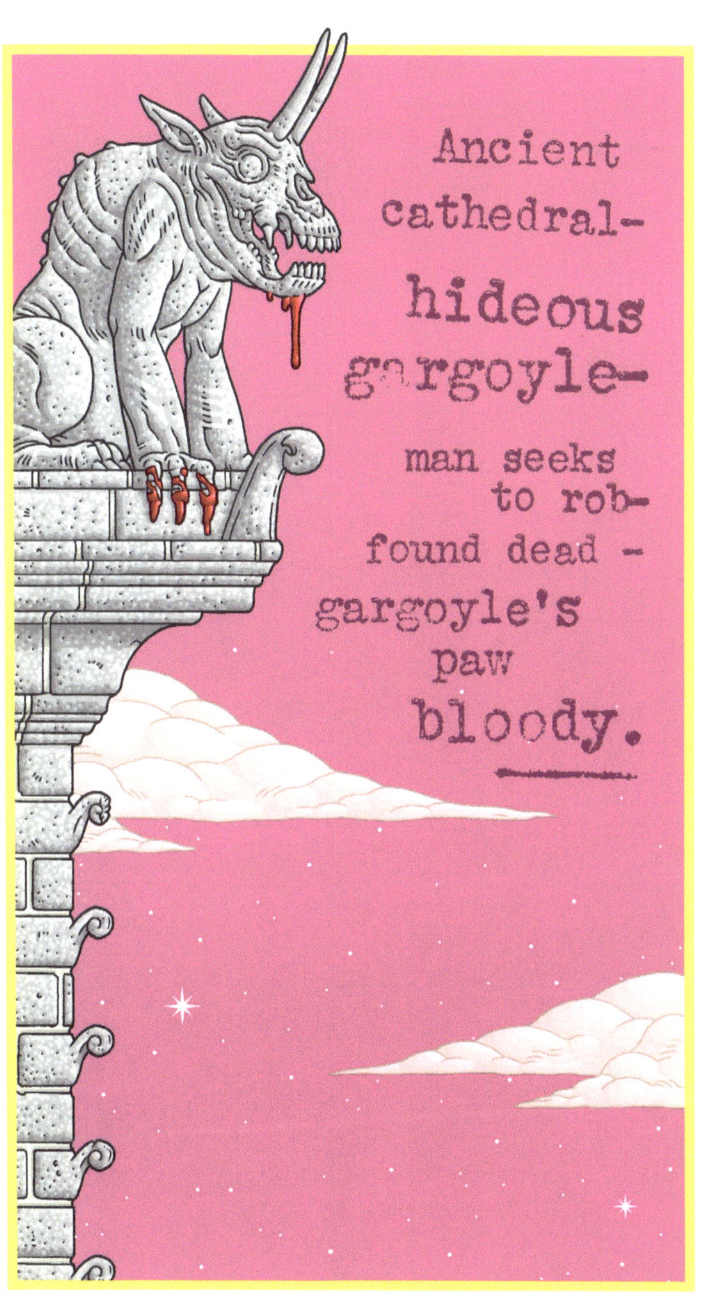

Ancient
cathedral—
hideous
gargoyle—
man seeks
to rob-
found dead —
gargoyle's
paw
bloody.

Salem story- the cottage of an
aged witch- wherein after her
death are found sundry terrible things.

        Subterranean region be-
      neath placid New England
village, inhabited by (living
 or extinct) creatures of
prehistoric antiquity &
strangeness.

Vampire visits man in ances-
tral abode- is his own father.

A thing that sat of a sleep-
er's chest. Gone in morning,
but something left behind.

    Old sea tavern now far
    inland from made land.

Happenings in interval between
preliminary sound & striking
of clock --ending-- "it was the
tones of the clock striking
                        three."

Horrible boarding house- clo-
    sed door never opened.

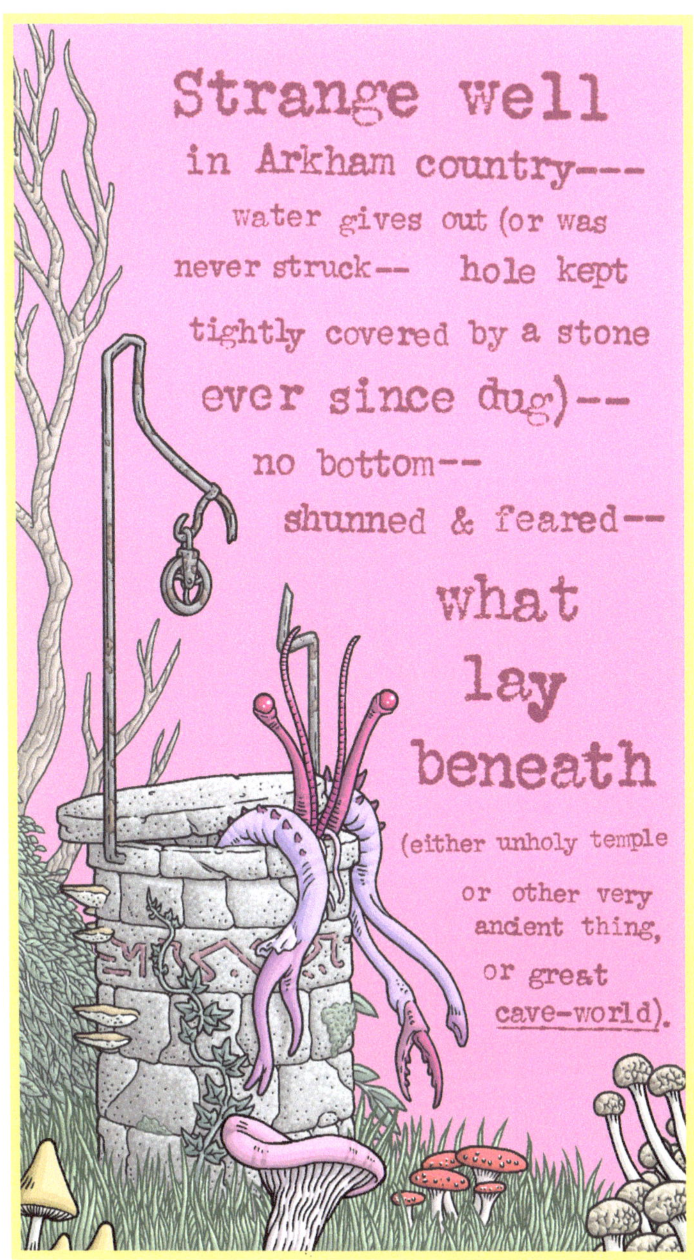

Strange well

in Arkham country---

water gives out (or was

never struck--   hole kept

tightly covered by a stone

ever since dug)--

no bottom--

shunned & feared--

what

lay

beneath

(either unholy temple

or other very
ancient thing,
or great
cave-world).

Ancient & unknown ruins--
strange & immortal bird who
speaks in a language horrify-
   ing & revelatory to the ex-
   plorers.

   Phosphorescence of decay-
ing wood- called in New England
" fox-fire".

In Ld Dunsany's "Idle Days on
the Yann" The inhabitants of
the antient Astahan, on the
Yann, do all things according
to antient ceremony. Nothing
new is found. "Here we have
fetter'd and manacled Time,
   who wou'd otherwise slay
                     the Gods."

   Secret language spoken by a
very few old men in wild
country leads to hidden marvels & horrors still surviving

   Prehistoric man preserved
in Siberian ice. (See Win-
chell Walks & Talks in the
Geological Field p156 et seq.)

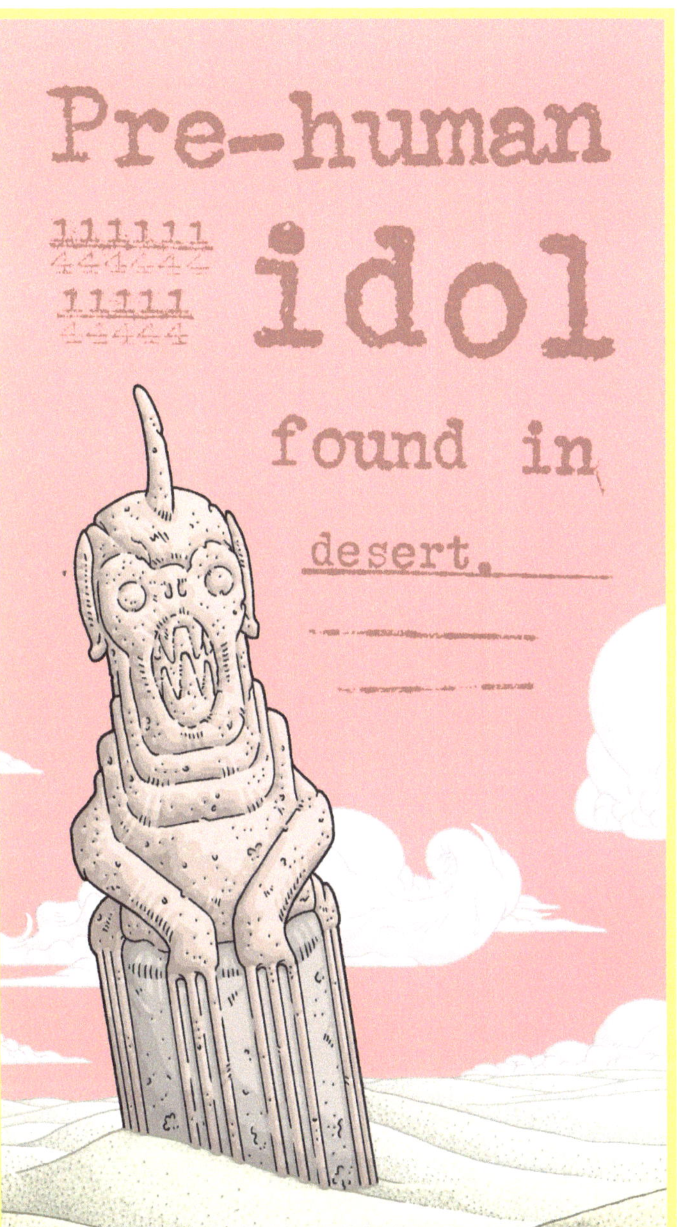

Pre-human
idol
found in
desert.

The <u>dreams</u> of one man actually <u>create</u> a strange half
mad world of quasi-material
substance in <u>another di-
mension.</u> Another man, also
a dreamer, blunders **into**
this world in a dream.
What he finds. Intelligence
of denizens. Their depen-
dence on the first dreamer.
<u>What happens at his death.</u>

Migrations of Lemmings...
<u>Atlantis.</u>

Little green
    Celtic figure
    dug up in an
    ancient Irish
<u>bog.</u>

A very ancient tomb
in the deep woods near
where a 17th Century Virginia
Manorhouse used to be. The <u>unde-
cayed, bloated thing found within.</u>

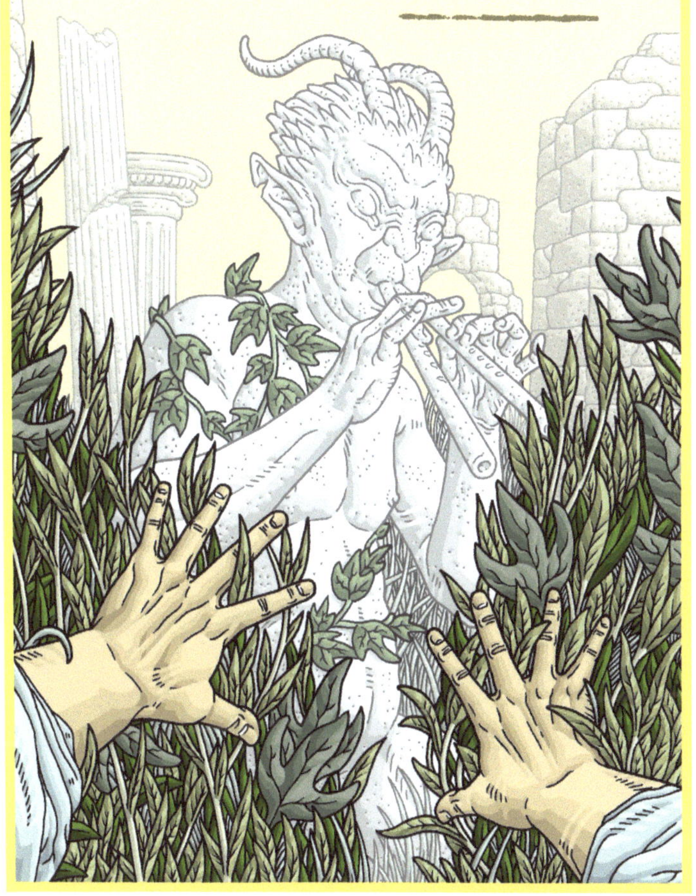

Marble Faun—
p 346. Strange &
prehistoric Italian
city of stone.

Ancient castle within sound
of weird waterfall- sound
ceases for a time under
strange conditions.

Mad artist in ancient sinister
house draws things. What were
his models? Glimpse.

Someone or something cries
in fright at sight of the
rising moon, as if it were
something strange.

Appearance of an ancient
god in a lonely & archaic
place- prob. temple ruin. Atmosphere of beauty rather tha
of horror. Subtle handling-
presence revealed by faint
sound or shadow. Landscape
changes ? Seen by child?

Impossible to reach or i-
dentify locale again ?

Halloween incident- mirror in
a cellar- face seen therein-
death (claw-mark ?)

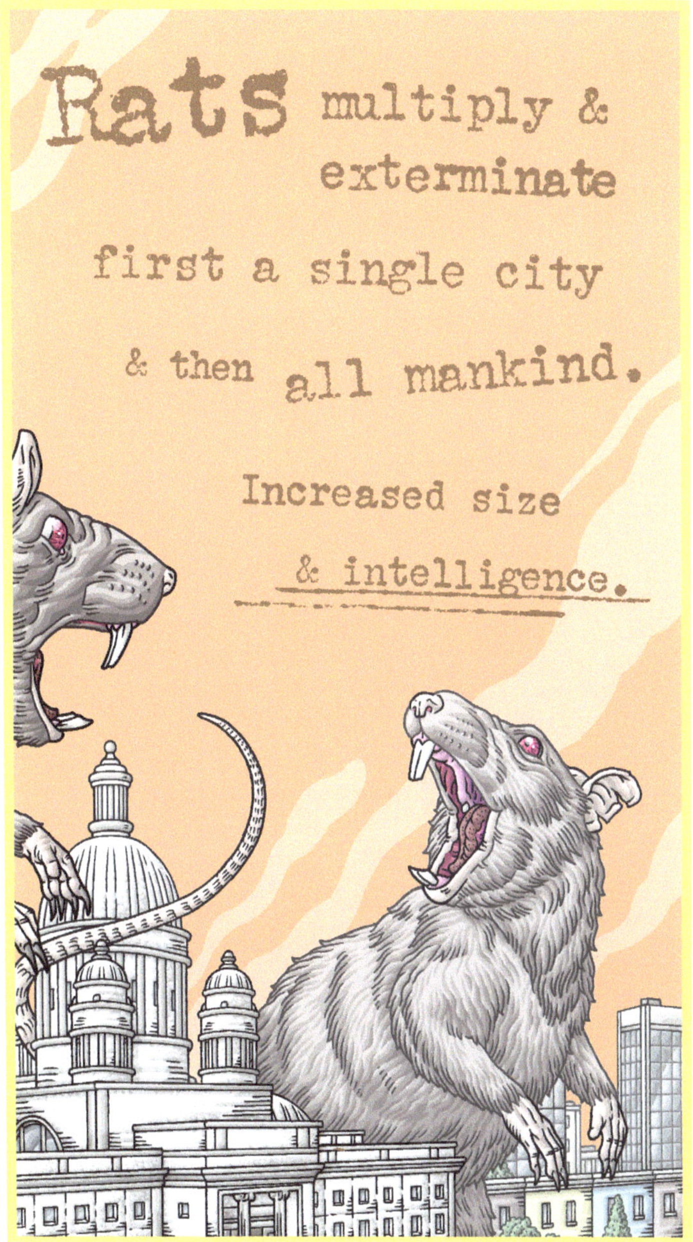

Rats multiply & exterminate first a single city & then all mankind.

Increased size & intelligence.

Rats multiply all mankind

A queer village - in a
valley , reached by a long
road & visible from the
crest of the hill from
which that road descends--
or close to a dense & an-
tique forest.

Live man buried in bridge
masonry according to super-
stition--or black cat.
    Riley's fear of under-
takers- door locked on inside
                    after death.

Vampire
dog

Hideous old
house
on steep
city hillside-Bowen St.-
beckons in the night-
black windows- horror un-
named- cold touch & voice-
the welcome of the dead.

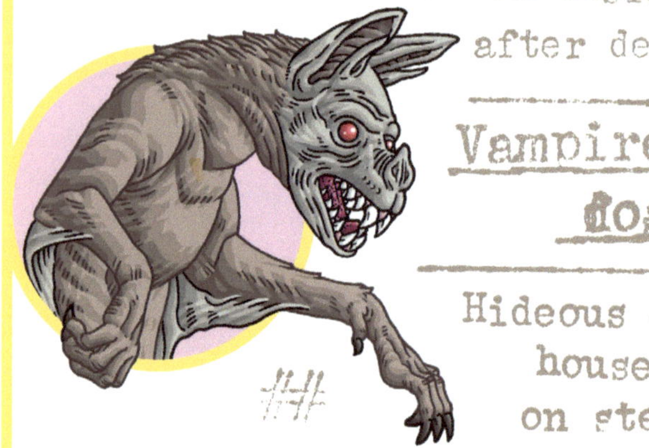

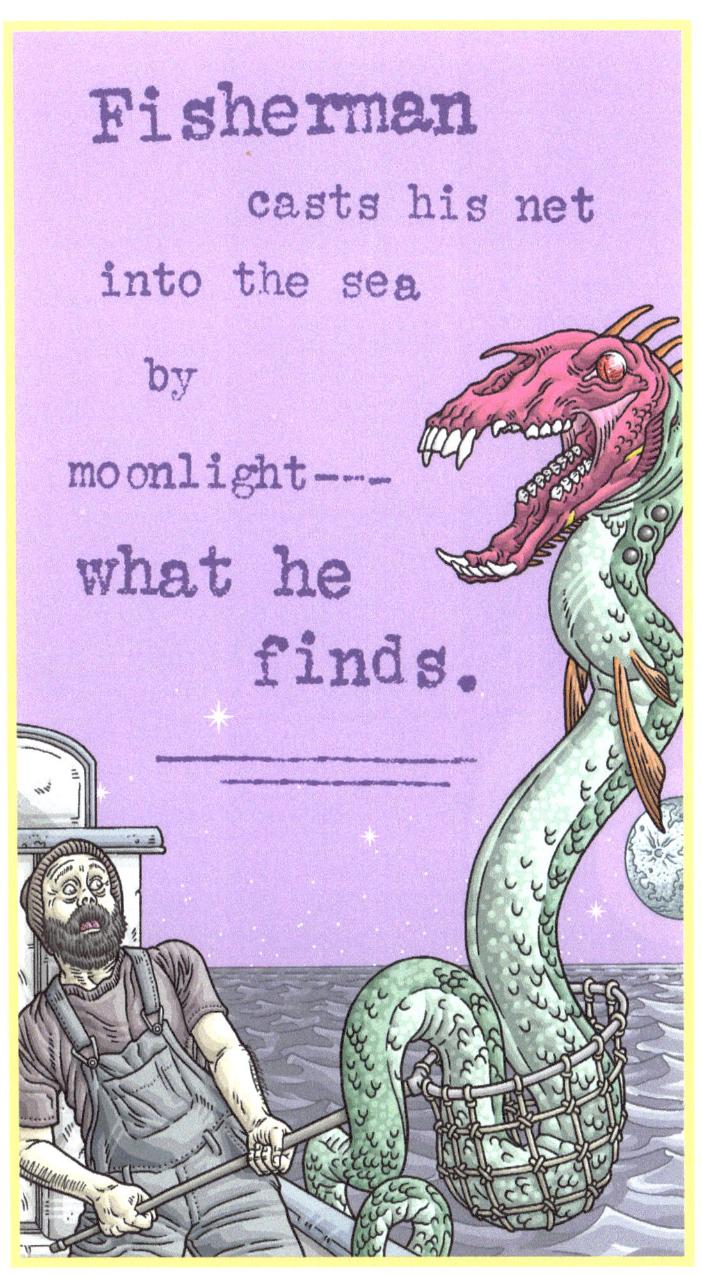

Fisherman
casts his net
into the sea
by
moonlight----
what he
finds.

Old sea tavern now
far inland from made land.
Strange occurrences- sound
of lapping of waves.

Man in strange subterranean
chamber- seeks to force door
of bronze- overwhelmed by in-
fluz of waters.   —

AZATHOTH--hideous name.

A terrible pilgrimage to
seek the nighted throne of
the far-daemon-sultan Aza-
thoth.

Sinister names--
Nasht-Kaman-Thah.

An impression- city in peril-
dead city-equestrian statue-
men in closed room-clattering
of hooves heard from outside
--marvel disclosed on
looking out - doubtful
ending.

Black Mass under antique
church.

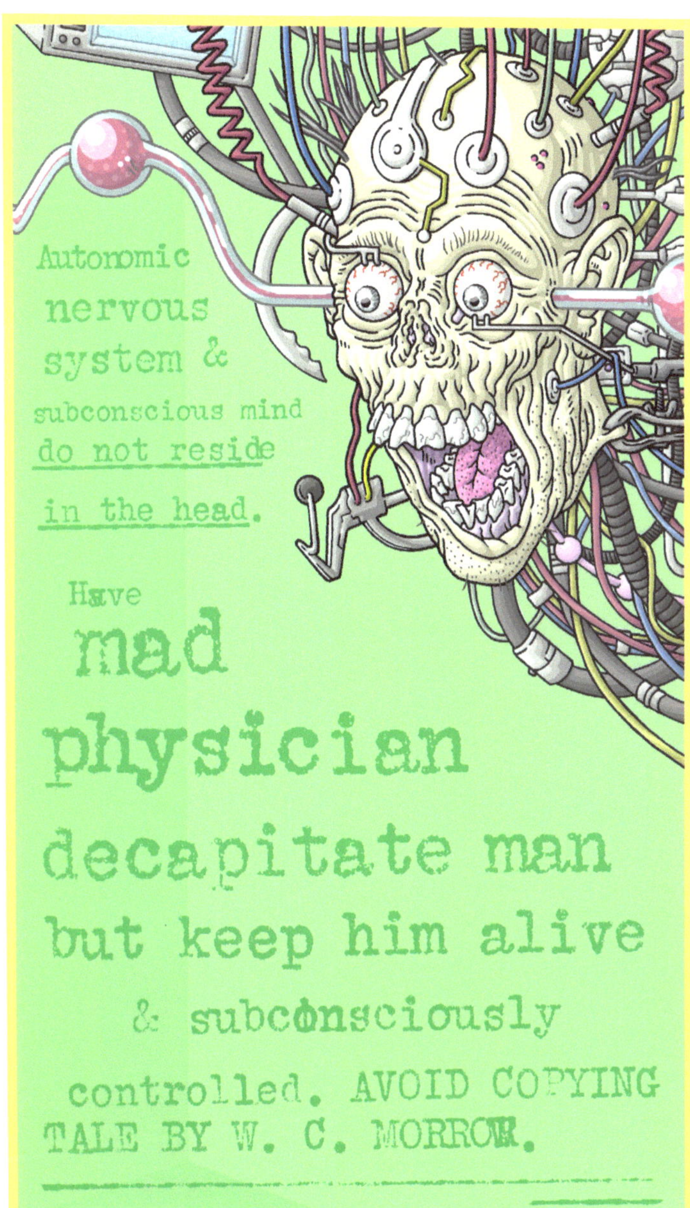

Autonomic nervous system & subconscious mind do not reside in the head.

Have mad physician decapitate man but keep him alive & subconsciously controlled. AVOID COPYING TALE BY W. C. MORROW.

Lonely philosopher fond of cat
Hypnotizes it-as it were- by
  repeatedly talking to it &
  looking at it. After his
  death the cat evinces signs of
his personality. He had trained
cat, & leaves it with friend,
  with instructions as to fit-
  ting a pen to its right fore-
paw by means of a harness-
later it writes with the
deceased's own handwriting.

  Book or manuscri t too horrible to read-warned against
  reading it- someone reads it
  & is found dead. Haverhill
  incident.

Sailing or rowing on lake
in moonlight- sailing into
invisible.

Enchanted garden where moon
casts shadow of object or
ghost invisible to human eye.

  Calling on the dead - voice
  or familiar sound in ad-
  jacent room.

Horrible secret in crypt
of ancient castle—discovered
by dweller.

Shapeless living thing forming nucleus of ancient build-
ing.

Power of wizard to influence
others.

"...a defunct nightmare, which
had perished in the midst
of its wickedness, & left
its flabby corpse on the breast
of the tormented one , to be
gotten rid of as it might."
                    ..Hawthorne.

Hideous cracked discords of
bass music from (ruined) organ
in (abandoned) abbey or
church.   Red Hook

" For has not nature, too, her
grotesques— the rent rock,
the distorted lights of
evening on lonely roads,
the unveiled structure of man
    in the embryo or the
    skeleton ?"
..Pater, Renaissance (da Vinci)

   Dream of ancient castle
stairs- sleeping guards-narrow
window- battle on plain
between men of England & men
of yellow tabards with red
dragons. Leader of English
challenges leader of foe to
single combat. They fight, foe
unhelmeted, but <u>there is no
head revealed</u>. Whole army of
foe fades into mist & watch
-er finds himself to be the
English knight on the plain,
mounted . Looks at castle <u>&</u>
sees a peculiar concentration
of fantastic clouds over the
 <u>highest battlements.</u>

   Visitor from tomb-stranger
at some public concourse
followed at midnight to grave-
yard where he descends into
the earth.

DELRIO asks "An sint unquam
 daemones incubi et succubae,
et an ex tali congressu
Red Hook proles nasci queat?"

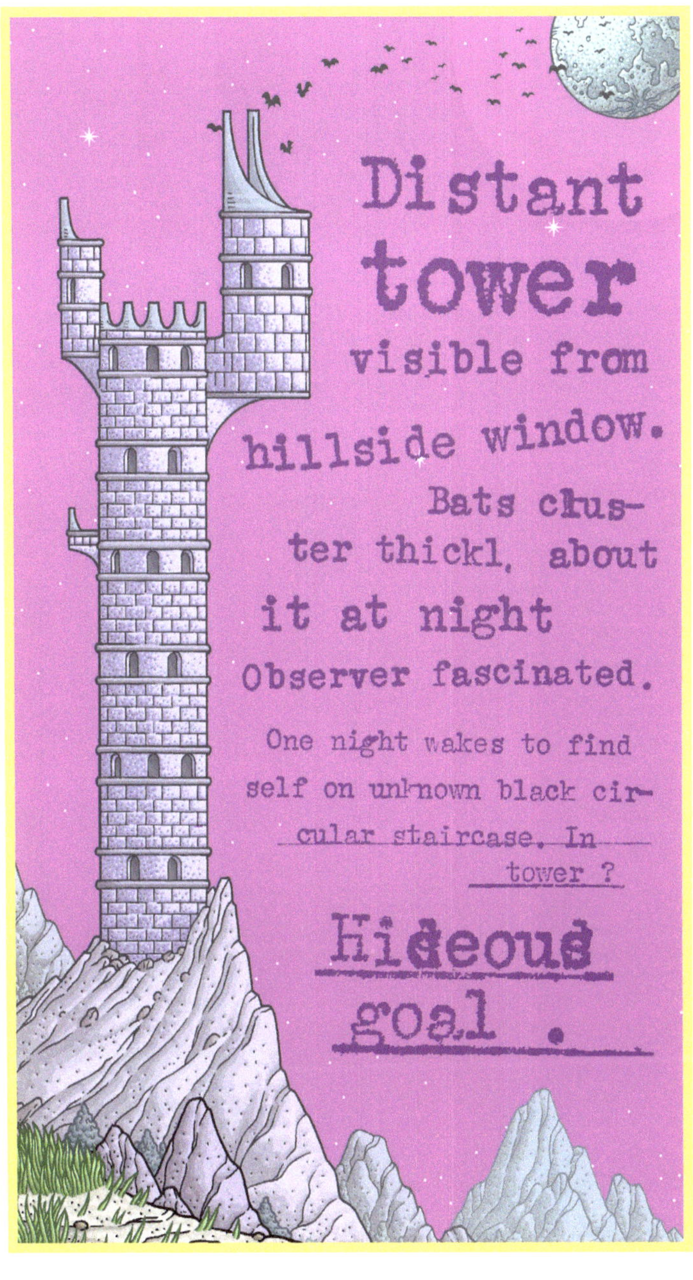

Distant tower visible from hillside window. Bats cluster thickl, about it at night Observer fascinated.
One night wakes to find self on unknown black circular staircase. In tower ?
Hideous goal .

Loss of memory & entry into
 a cloudy world of strange
sights & experiences after
shock, accident, reading
of strange book, participation
in strange rite, draught of
 strange brew &c. Things seen
 have vague & disquieting fa-
mliarity, Emergence. Inability
to retrace course.

A general house of horror-
nameless crime- sounds-
later tenants- (Flamm-
 arion) (novel length ?)

Transposition of
 identity.

Daemons, when
desiring an human
form for
evil purposes, take
to themselves the
 bodies of hanged men.

Peculiar odour of a book of
childhood induces repitition
of childhood fancy.

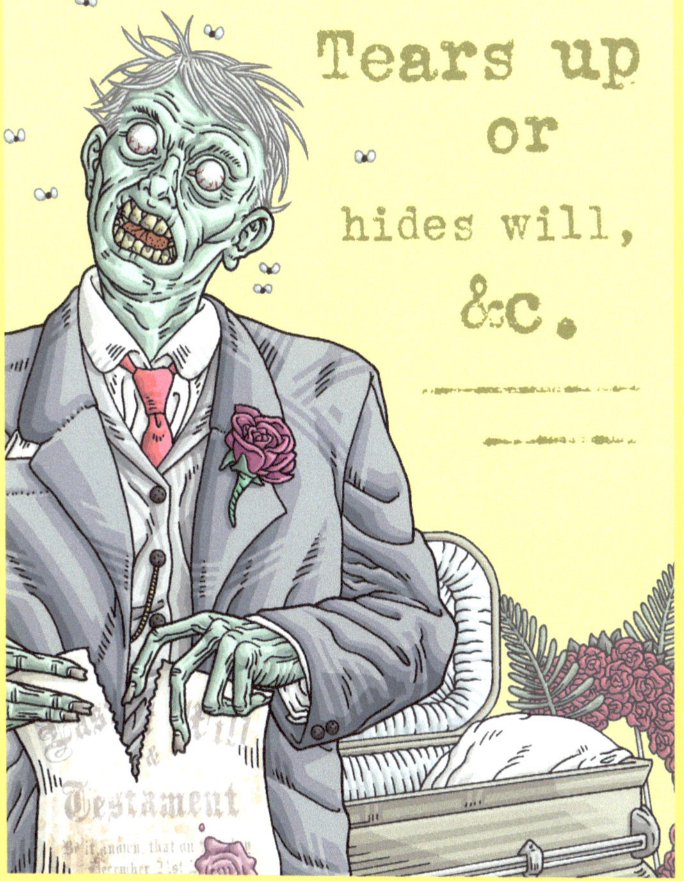
Corpse in room
performs some act—
prompted by discussion
in its presence.
Tears up
or
hides will,
&c.

Hideous family living in
    shadow in ancient castle
        by edge of wood near
black cliffs & monstrous
waterfall.

Boy reared in atmosphere of
considerable mystery. Be-
lieves father dead. Suddenly is told father is about
        to return. Strange pre-
parations - consequences.

    Strange man in shadowy
quarter of ancient city
    possesses something of
immemorial archaic horr-
or.

    Idol in museum moves in
    a certain way.

Biological or hereditary memor-
ies of other worlds & universes. / Butler- God Known &
Unk. p 59 /

Death lights dancing over a
salt marsh.

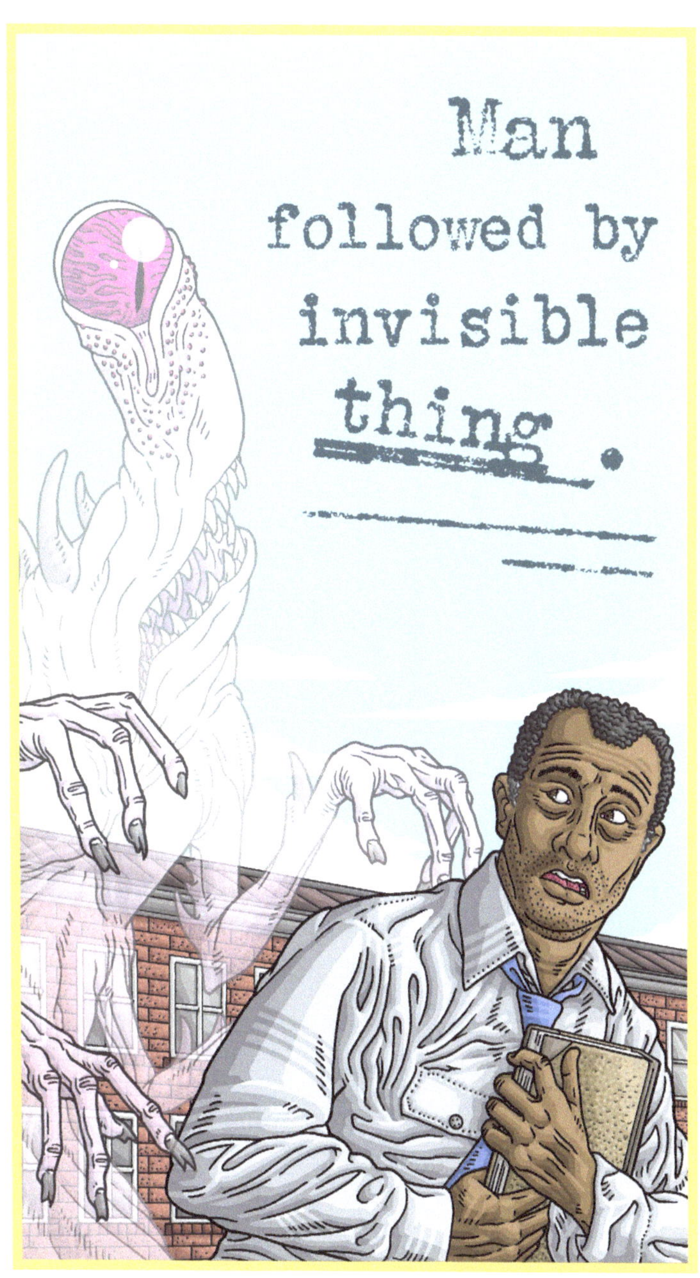
Man
followed by
invisible
thing .

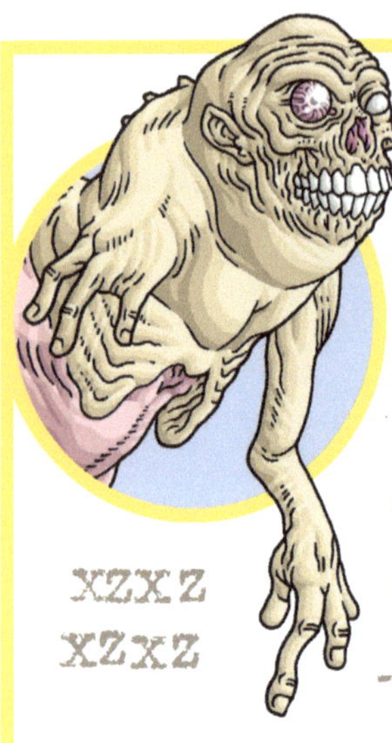

Man has miniature
shapeless Siamese
twin-   exhibit in
circus-
twin surgically de-
tatched disappears-
does hideous thing
s/ with malign life
of its own.

XZXZ
XZXZ

Doors found mysteriously
open & shut & excites terro

Narrator walks along un-
familiar country road,-
comes to region of the
unreal.

Man journeys into the past
or imaginative realm----
leaving bodily shell behind.

House & garden---old
associations. Scene takes
on strange aspect in the
dark.

Hideous sound in the dark.

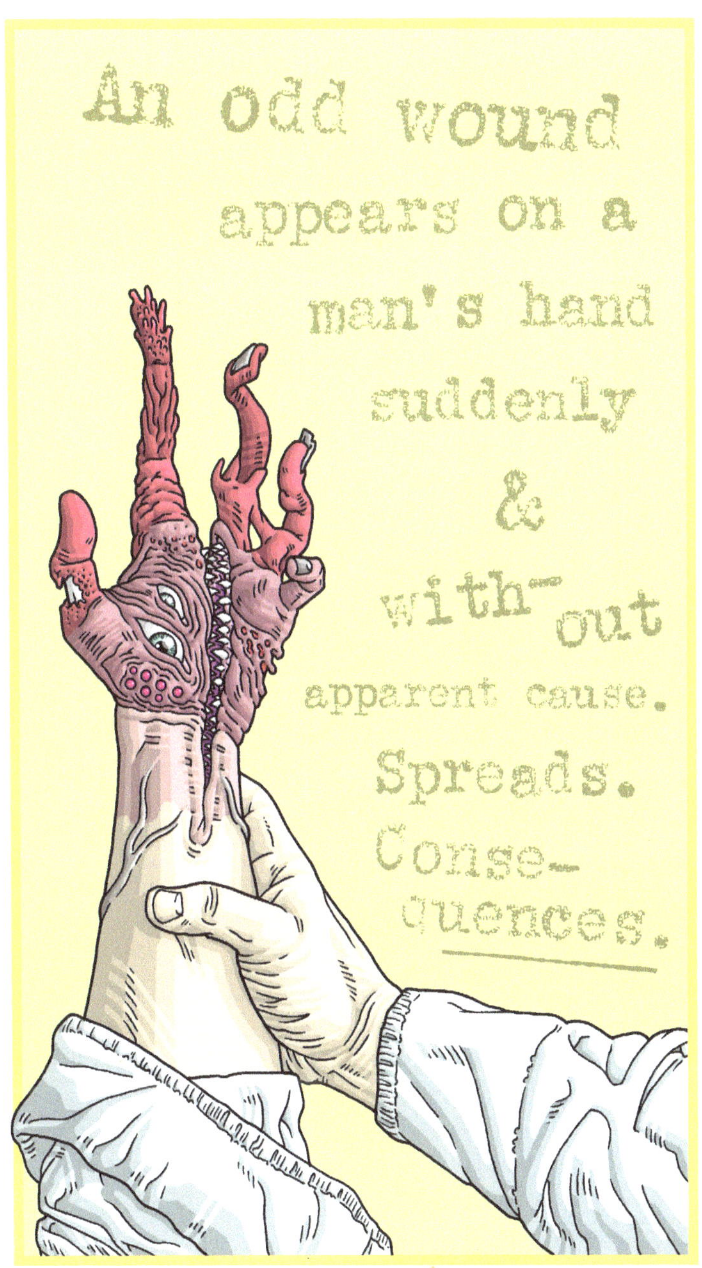

An odd wound appears on a man's hand suddenly & without apparent cause. Spreads. Consequences.

Person gazes out window &
finds city & world dark & dead
  (or oddly changed) outside.

Trying to identify & visit the
distant scenes dimly seen from
one's window--bizarre consequences.

Something snatched away from
one in the dark--in a lonely,
ancient, & generally shunned
  place.

An ancient house with black-
ened pictures on the walls--so
obscured that their subjects
cannot be deciphered. Clean-
ing-- & revelation. Cf.
Hawthorne-Edw. Rand. Port.

Begin story with presence of
  narrator--inexplicable to
himself--in utter.ly alien &
terrifying scenes (dream?).

Ancient winter woods--moss
--greatK boles--twisted
branches--dark-ribbed roots
--always dripping ...

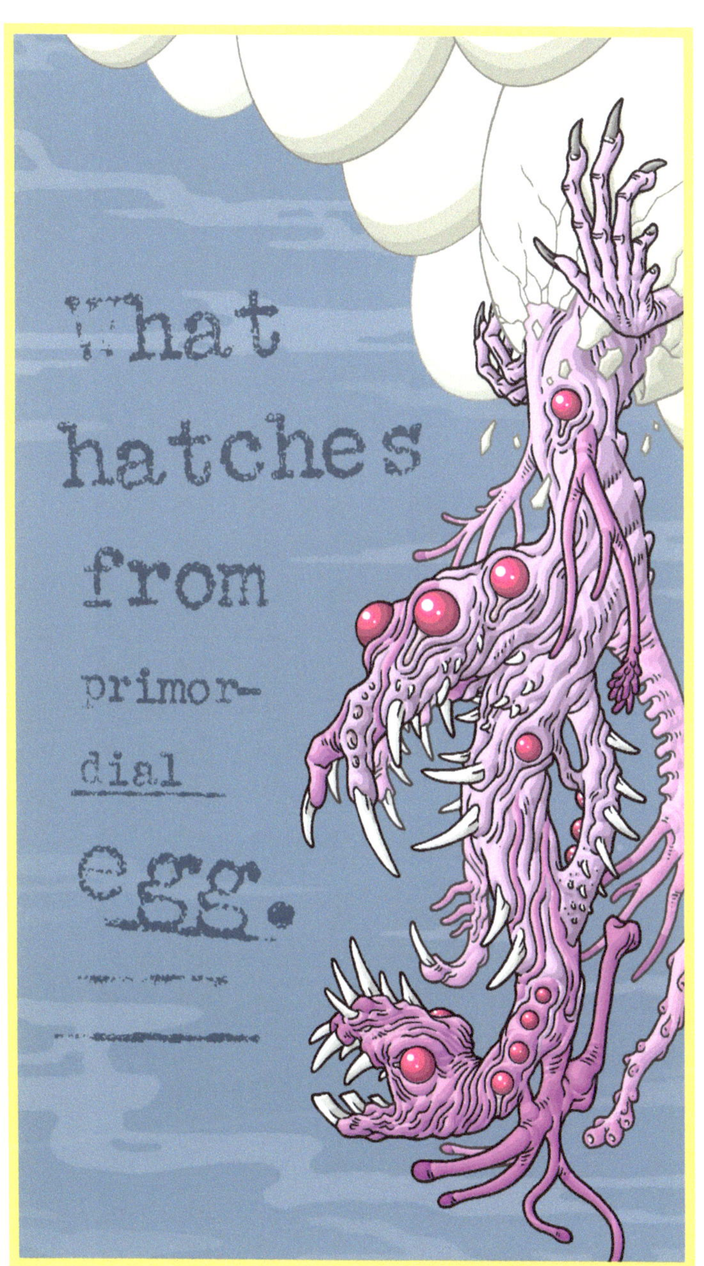
...that

hatches

from

primor-
dial

egg.

Special Correspondence of NY
Times-March 3, 1935 "Halifax,
N.S.-Etched deeply into the
face of an island which rises
from the Atlantic surges off the
S. coast of Nova Scotia 20 m.
from Halifax is the strangest
rock phenomenon which Canada
boasts. Storm, sea, & frost have
graven into the solid cliff of
what has come to be known as
Virgin's Island an almost
perfect outline of the Madonna
with the Christ Child in her
arms. The island has sheer &
wave-bound sides, is a danger
to ships,& is absolutely unin-
habited. So far as is known, no
human being has ever set foot
on its shores."

Strange human being (or
    beings) living in some
ancient house or ruins
far from populous district
(either old N.E. or far
    exotic land). Suspicion
(based on shape and habits)
that it is not all human.

Castaways on island
eat unknown vegeta-
tion & become
strangely
transformed.
____

Inhabitants of
Zinge, over whom
the star Canopus rises
every night, are always gay
& without sorrow.
____

Individual , by some strange
process, retraces the path
of evolution & becomes amphib-
ious.
Dr. insists that the partic-
ular amphibian form from which
man descends is not like any
known to palaeontology. To
prove it indulges in (or
relates) strange experiment.
____

The shores of Attica respond
in song to the waves of the
Aegean.
____

Ancient necropolis -bronze
door in hillside which opens
as the moonlight strikes it-
focussed by ancient lens in
pylon opposite

Invisible Thing felt-
    or seen to make prints-
on mountain top or other
high inaccessible place.

Black winged thing flies into one's house at night.Can-
not be found, or identified-
but subtle developements
            ensue.

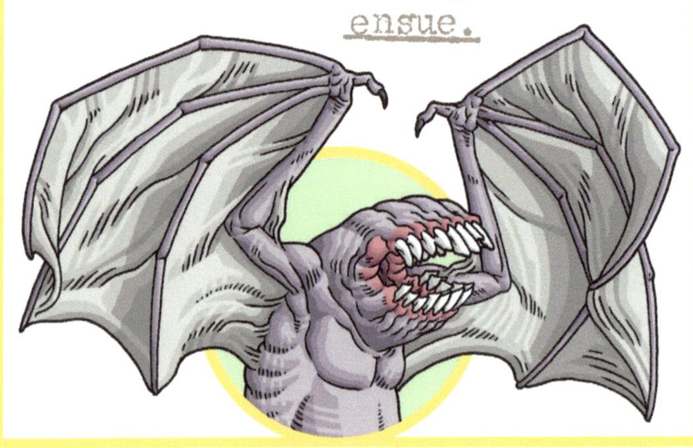

Hideous world superimposed on
visible world- gate through-
power guides narrator to ancient & forbidden book with
directions for access.

Disintegration of all matter
to electrons & finally empty
space assured, just as devol-
urion of energy to radiant
heat is known. Case if accel-
eration---man passes into
space.

Dr. Eben Spencer plot.

Explorer enters strange
land where some atmospheric
quality darkens sky to vir-
tual blackness- marvels there-
in.

Members of witch-cult were
buried face downward. Man
investigates ancestor in family
vault & finds disquiet-
ing condition.

Hideous book glimpsed in ancient shop - never seen again.

Drowning sensations -under-
sea- ships- souls of the dead
Drowning is a horrible death.

Horror Story Man dreams of
falling-- found on floor mangled
as tho' from falling from a

                          vast height.
____

Warning that certain ground
is sacred or accursed; that a
house or city must not be
built upon it or must be de-
stroyed or abandoned if built
under penalty of catastrophe.

    Fear of mirrors—memory of
    dream in which scene is al-
tered & climax is hideous
surprise at seeing oneself in
the water or mirror. (Identity.?)
____

Castle by pool or river---
    reflection fixed thro'
centuries- castle destroyed-
    reflection lives to avenge
    destroyers weirdly.
____

64

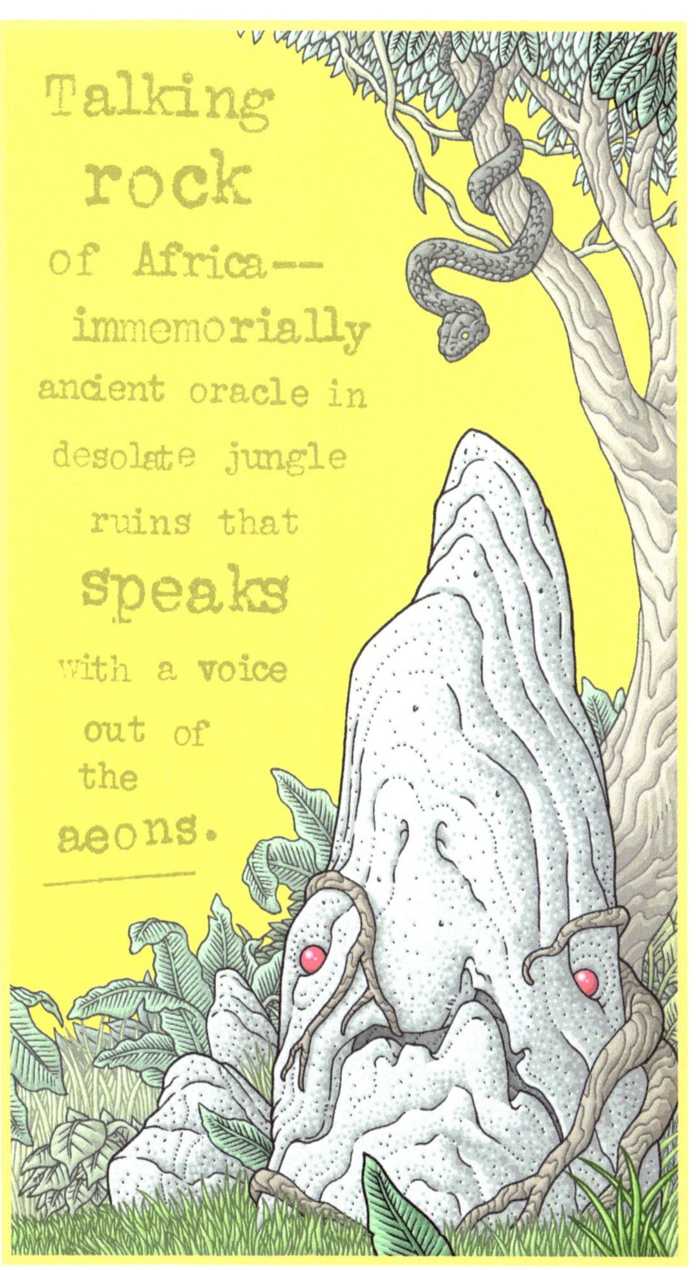

Talking
rock
of Africa--
immemorially
ancient oracle in
desolate jungle
ruins that
speaks
with a voice
out of
the
aeons.

To find something horrible in
  a(perhaps familiar) book,&
not to be able to find it
again.

Marblehead--dream--burying
  hill--evening--unreality.

  Catacombs discovered beneath a city. (in
  America?)

Black cat on hill near dark
gulf of ancient inn yard. Mews
  hoarsely- invites artist to
  nighted mysteries beyond. Finally dies at advanced age.
Haunts dreams of artist- lures
  him to follow- strange outcome
(never wake up ? or make
bizarre discovery of an el-
der world outside three-dimen-
sion space ?)

  Horrible Colonial farmhouse
  & overgrown garden on city
  hillside-- overtaken by
growth. Verse "The House"
  as basis of story.

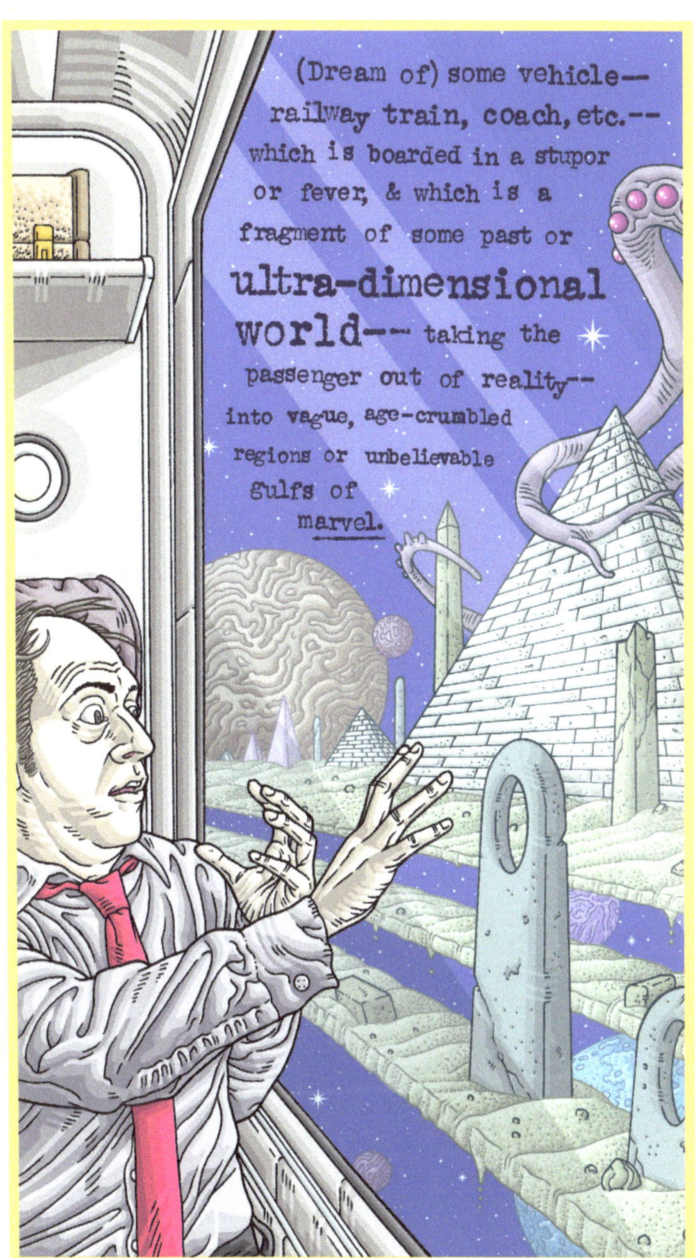

(Dream of) some vehicle--
railway train, coach, etc.--
which is boarded in a stupor
or fever, & which is a
fragment of some past or
ultra-dimensional
world--- taking the
passenger out of reality--
into vague, age-crumbled
regions or unbelievable
gulfs of
marvel.

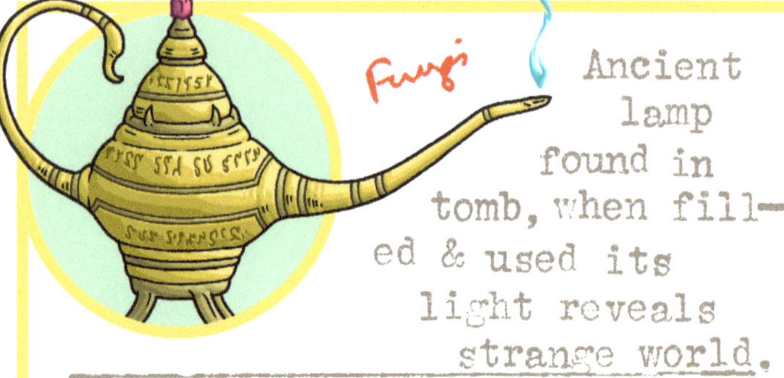

Ancient
lamp
found in
tomb, when fill-
ed & used its
light reveals
strange world.

Man with lost memory in strange,
imperfectly comprehended
environment. Fear to regain
memory--a glimpse.

Bell of some ancient church or
castle rung by some unknown hand--
a thing...or an invisible Presence.

Ancient (Roman? prehistoric?)
stone bridge washed away by a
(sudden & curious?) storm. Something
liberated which had been sealed up
in the masonry of years ago.
Things happen.

Man idly shapes queer image--
power impels him to make it
queerer than he understands.
Throws it away in disgust-- But
something abroad in the night.

From ARABIA Ency. Britan.
   II 255
   Prehistoric fabulous tribes
of Ad in the south, Thamood
in the north, & Tasm & Jadis
in the centre of the penin-
sula. "Very gorgeous are the
   descriptions given of Irem,
   the City of Pillars (as
   the Koran styles it)
supposed to have been erected
by Shedad, the latest despot
of Ad, in the regions of Had-
ramant, & which yet, after
the annihilation,of its ten-
ants, remains entire so Arabs
   say, invisible to the
ordinary eyes, but occasionally & at rare intervals,
   revealed to some heaven-
favoured traveller." //Rock
excavations in N.W. Hejaz
ascribed to Thamood tribe.

Race of immortal Pharaohs
dwelling beneath pyramids
   in vast subterranean halls
down black staircases.

Hideous old book discovered
with directions for shock-
ing evocation.

Antedéluvian - cyclopean ruins
on lonely Pacific island-
Centre of earthwide subterranean witch cult.

    Ancient ruin in Alabama
swamo- voodoo.

Man lives near graveyard- how
does he live ?- Eats no food.

Prowling at night around an
unlighted castle amidst
strange scenery.

    Hideous secret assemblage
    at night in antique alley-
disperse furtively one by
one- one seen to drop some-
thing- a human hand.

ART NOTE- fantastick
    daemons of
Salvator
Rosa or   Fuseli.
(/ Trunk-
    proboscis)/

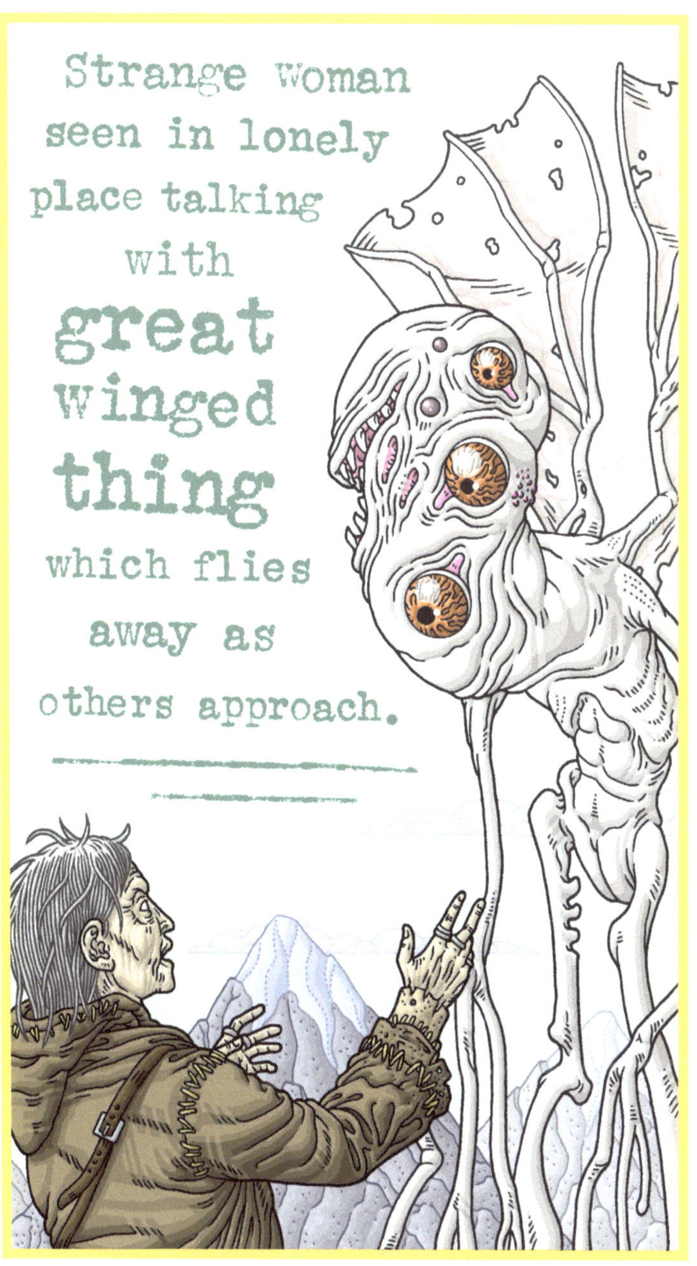

Strange woman
seen in lonely
place talking
with
great
winged
thing
which flies
away as
others approach.

Reference in Egyptian papyrus to a secret of secrets
under tomb of high-priest
Ka-Nefer. Tomb finally found
 & identified--trap door in
stone floor--staircase, &
the illimitable black abyss.

A monstrous derelict--found &
   boarded by a castaway or
shipwreck survivor.

Disturbing conviction that all
life is only a deceptive dream
with some dismal or sinister
horror lurking behind.

A return to a place under dreamlike,
 horrible, & only dimly comprehended
      circumstances. Death & decay
reigning-- town fails to light up at
                    night-- Revelation.

Mirage in time--image of long-
vanish'd pre-human city.

Fog or smoke--assumes shapes
          under incantations.

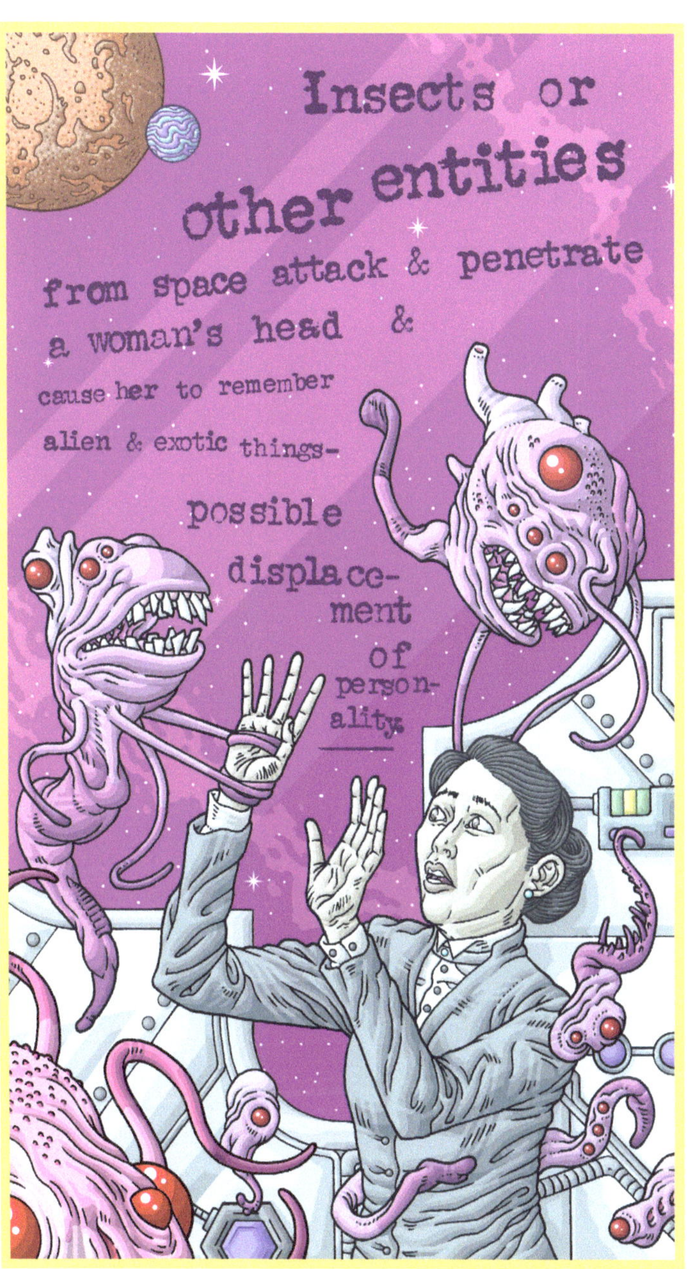

Insects or
other entities
from space attack & penetrate
a woman's head &
cause her to remember
alien & exotic things—
possible
displace-
ment
of
person-
ality.

Steepled town seen from afar
  at sunset- does not light up
at night. Sail has been seen
 putting out to sea.   *Fungi*

Adventures of a disembodied
spirit- thro' dim, half-famil-
iar cities & over strange
moors- thro' space & time-
other planets & universes in
the end

Vague lights, geometrical fig-
ures, &c seen on retina when
  eyes are closed. Caused by
rays from other dimensions act
-ing on optic nerves ? From
other planets ? Connected
with a life or phase of being
in which person could live if
he only knew how to get there?
 Man afraid to shut eyes ----
he has been somewhere on a
  terrible pilgrimage & this
fearsome seeing faculty
remains.

  Planets formed of invisi-
     ble matter.

Tone of extreme phantasy
    Man transformed to island
or mountain

As dinosaurs were once sur-
    passed by mammals, so will
man-mammal be surpassed by in-
sect or bird--fall of man be-
    fore the new race.

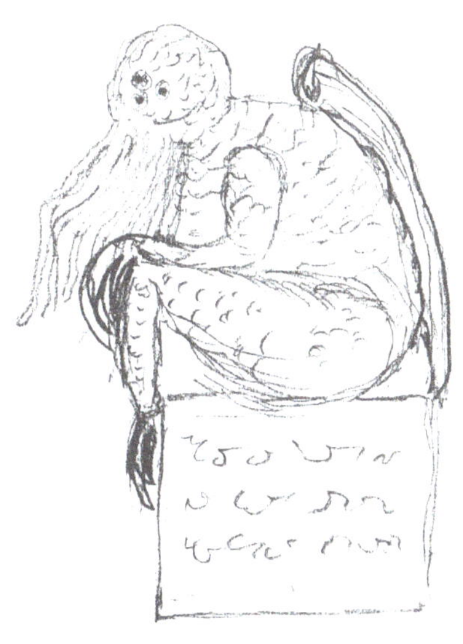

To R. H. Barlow, Esq., whose Sculpture
hath given Immortality to this trivial
Design of his oblig'd obt Servt
                    Cthulhu
                            H. P. Lovecraft
11th May, 1934

ひひひひひひひひひひひひひひひひひひひひひひひひひひひひ
Books to mention in new
edition of weird article
ひひひひひひひひひひひひひひひひひひひひひひひひひひひひ

R.E.Spencer- The Lady who Came
to Stay. (1931)

H.B.Drake-The Shadowy Thing (1928)

John Buchan- Witch Wood (1927)

Herbert S. Gorman - The Place
Called Dagon. (1927)

Leonard Cline-Dark Chamber (1927)

E.F.Benson - The Face-in Spook
Stories

Sinister House by Leland Hall
(1919)

Arthur Ransome-The Elixir of
Life (1915)

. . . .

William Hope
Hodgson

The Boats Of
'Glen Carrig'
(1907)

The Ghost
Pirates (1909)

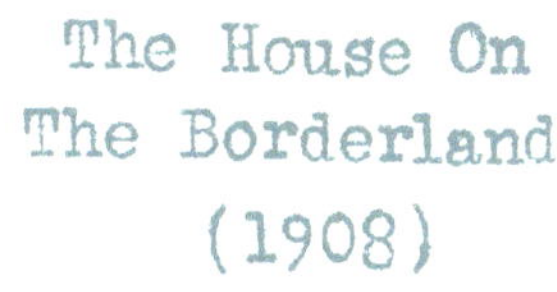

Carnacki, The Ghost Finder
(1913)

The House On
The Borderland
(1908)

The Night Land
(1912)

. . . .

George Macdonald-
Lilith (1895)

Barry Pain- The
Undying Thing
(1901)

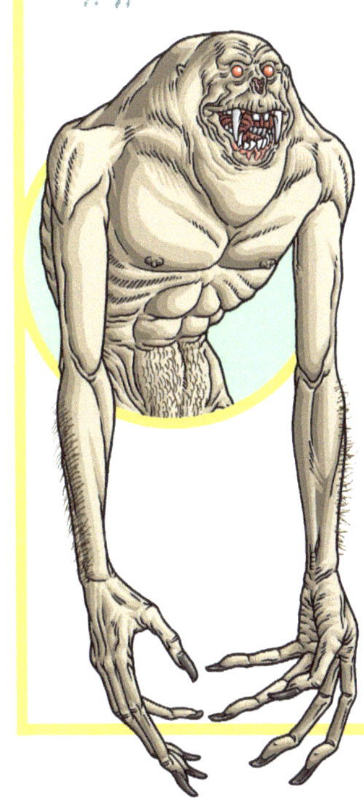

James Hogg—Memoirs of a Justi-
fied Sinner & others

Mrs. H. D. Everett- Short Sto-
ries.(Post-war)
· · · · · · ·
H.R. Wakefield
"THEY RETURN AT EVENING" (1928)

He Cometh & He Passeth By

The Red Lodge

The Seventeenth Hole
at Duncaster

And He Shall Sing

H.R. Wakefield
"OTHERS WHO RETURNED" (1929)

The Cairn

Look Up There

Blind Man's Buff
· · · · · · ·
John Buchan- Runagates Club
The Green Wildebeest
The Wind in the Portico
Skule Skerry

· · · · · · ·
Short St. ASQUITH'S GHOST BOOK
(1927)
Algernon Blackwood- Chemical
Hugh Walpole- Mrs Lunt
L.P.Hartley- A Visitor From
Down Under

Walter De la Mare- A Recluse
· · · · · · ·
Short Stories from French's
GHOSTS GRIM & GENTLE
(1926)
H.G.Wells The Ghost of Fear
Guy de Maupassant- On the River
Ralph Adams Cram-The Dead
Valley

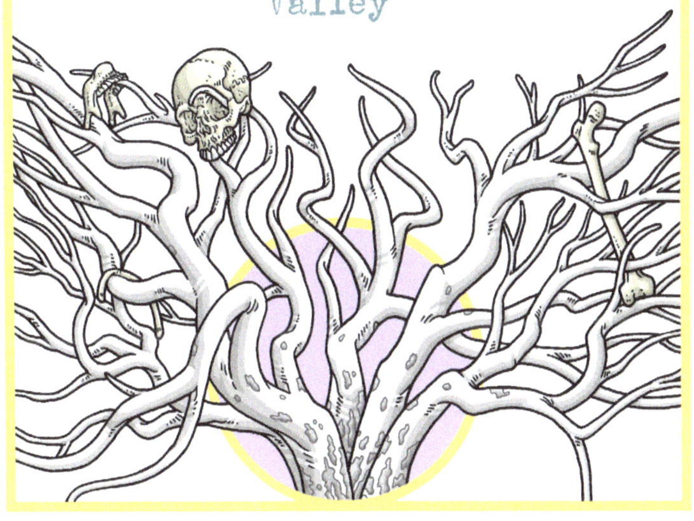

ARTIST'S NOTES

There are two **versions of Lovecraft's Commonplace** Book. The first **is** his handwritten copy, which was given to R.H. Barlow, who then **created** the second typewritten copy. In the handwritten version, Lovecraft **crossed** out entries he **expanded** into stories or were too similar to **previous** entries. I've combined both **versions** here **&** included **some** of Lovecraft's handwritten notes **in red.**

Two entries have been **redacted** because of racist language **&** bigoted stereotypes.

While some entries in the handwritten copy were dated, the dates themselves are inconsistent; i.e., the **first few** pages aren't dated **&** entries from 1928 appear before entries from 1924. Since these are scattershot ideas meant to inspire, I've chosen to present them in random order.

His Commonplace Book also included a

list of stories he planned to mention
in his Supernatural Horror in Litera-
ture. I've included this list in blue
typeface towards the end of the book.

Right before the list is a sketch of
Cthulu. This was done by Lovecraft him
self & presented to Barlow just days
after he gave him the Commonplace Book
to transcribe.

Almost all the text is as it appears in
the typewritten copy. The only changes
I made were to change the pronouns of a
few characters. This was simply because
Lovecraft almost always wrote from the
perspective of a white man. As an artist, I found drawing the same type of
people boring, hence the changes.

My cover for this book is a loving re
ference to those early D&D supplements,
specifically the work of the talented
Erol Otus, after having the full text
of the Commonplace Book churn in my
brain for almost a year.

Thank you to Amol Ray & Stu Horvath for typing entries for me. Thanks to Alex Eckman-Lawn, Alan Brown & Alice Doyle for critiquing this work in progress. Thanks to Roxy & Sean for feeding me & keeping me sane. Thank you to my amazingly **talented, thought**ful & inspirational partner **Jeanne D'Angelo**. She talked me down when I was freaking out & always boosted my confidence when I needed it. And thanks to Steve Berman for his patience as this project **transformed into a beast** that **took** way longer than it should have.

For Vinegar Vincent Price, a prince of Ulthar & my best boy.

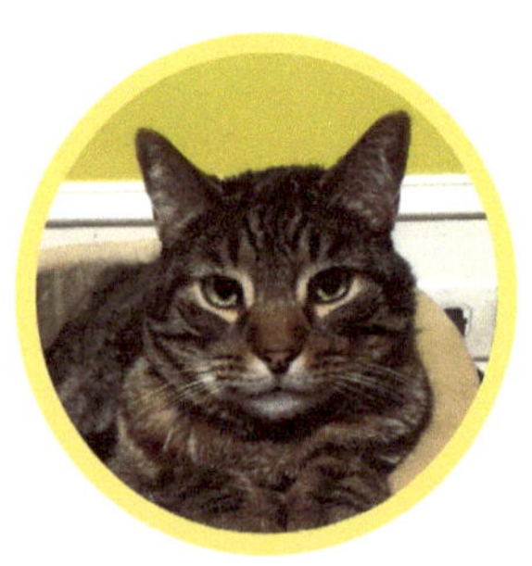